THE TREBORS

Trebor Tales, Book 1

CAROLINE C. BARNEY

Relax. Read. Repeat.

The Trebors (Trebor Tales, Book 1)
By Caroline C. Barney
Published by TouchPoint Press
Brookland, AR 72417
www.touchpointpress.com

ISBN-13: 978-1-946920-99-7

Editor: Jenn Haskin
Cover Design: Colbie Myles
Cover images: Árbol gigante by anibal (Adobe Stock); Perfect mountain sunset, orange pink sunset on uninhabited island. 3d procedural generated landscape by Anastasiia (Adobe Stock)
Map image design: Michael William Aldinger

Visit the author's website at carolinebarney.com

First Edition

Printed in the United States of America.

To my remarkable daughters, Madeline and Lucy, I love you endlessly.

Mt. Bor

Foothills

Nidus Landing

Borian Sea

CHAPTER 1

The tree shook violently. The winds and rain rushed through its branches, bending, pulling, and twisting its limbs. Stella's chest tightened and her fingers tingled. She took a deep breath and tried to calm her nerves as she clung tightly to her family. With her eyes squeezed shut Stella attempted to block out the terror of the storm by thinking of the quiet from the day before. The gentle winds had meant a cooler evening with the dancing and singing of the other Trebors. She wished she could go back and take part this time. But even as she tried to distract herself with these thoughts, the howling winds and screaming voices forced Stella to open her eyes. The tingling in her hands returned and crept up her arms and down her spine. She shuddered and slid her knees in more closely to her mother. Her younger brother, Ebert, lay on her mother's lap, tucked into a tight ball with his blanket looped around his pinkie finger and pressed against his face.

"Shhhh... shhhh... it'll end soon," her mother whispered into Ebert's ear. She wrapped her arm around Stella's knees and pulled her closer as she spoke to Ebert. Stella let herself rest against her mother's embrace, her warm body soothing the twitching that bristled Stella's fur. Ebert whimpered again and Stella lay her head on top of his long, curly, blond hair. She ran her fingers in circles along the fur on his arm, trying to bring him some comfort. The floor they sat on shook as the wind howled and Ebert only moaned more loudly. She dropped her hand from his arm and sat up straight to look directly at her mother.

"Yama, what if the tree can't hold?" Stella whispered.

"The tree will hold. Remember, our tribe has lived here for hundreds of years. Its roots are strong and most of our homes are built within the trunk, where it is the strongest… it will hold," Yama replied.

Stella felt annoyed by the thinness in her mother's voice and by another answer that her mother certainly doubted herself. She was twelve now, she didn't need her mother to protect her from the truth. She shook her head, pulled away from her mother, and slid a few feet away from them. The roaring wind shook the tree again and she pressed her back against the wall to steady herself. A sudden flash of lightening lit the inside of the tree. The bright explosion bounced off of something swinging violently back and forth in the corner of her home. Stella squinted to focus her eyes. It was her father's pouch, the one he usually wore around his neck. There was no mistaking its long, worn, leather string, with the tiny cloth pouch dangling at the bottom. The pouch swung so vigorously that Stella was surprised she hadn't noticed it before. *Why didn't her father have it with him?* She thought. *He always carried it on him.* Yet, there it was dangling from a hook in the tree's bark. She had to get to the pouch to save it from flying off the hook and getting lost.

Slowly, Stella pushed herself up to her feet. She stood with her arms wide and her knees bent, but the tree lurched and sent her crashing back to her knees. She peered back at her mother, but the sound of the storm had blocked the noise of her fall. Her mother was too busy comforting Ebert to notice what Stella was doing. Once again, she pushed herself to her feet, and when she was able to stand, she took a small step. Emboldened by this small progress, she took a larger step and then another. She reached her arm towards the pouch, but the tree heaved again. She was knocked off her feet and landed hard on her knee once more. A sharp pain ran through her leg. Yama grabbed Stella's forearm and pulled hard. Stella slid across the floor back to where her mother and Ebert sat, the force of her mother's grip left no room for alternatives.

"Why won't you stay still and listen to me? You can't go anywhere. The tree is doing the work. There is nothing we can do. Stop making this harder than it already is!" Yama hissed.

Stella gave in to her mother's grasp and crumbled against her brother. She sat in silence rubbing the exposed skin on her knee where the fur had torn off. The pouch swung back and forth, back and forth. Her heart seemed to beat in rhythm with the swinging pouch, its pattern harsh, quick, and erratic. The wind howled and the tree groaned. Branches snapped as the wind pulled limbs from the tree's trunk. The pouring rain grew louder outside, echoing in the hollow core of the tree. Lightning came in fits and bursts, blinding Stella with its glare. The thunder was deafening.

"We had signs that the storm was brewing on the other side of Mt. Bor weeks ago… why couldn't we do more to prepare?"

she yelled to her mother. "How can you all be so sure that the tree is going to hold… and Yapa… Yapa…he just left us here in the tree with nothing to help us fight against the storm. Why would he and the other elders leave like that?" She was angry and her voice betrayed her emotions.

The blood rose in her mother's checks, the pink hue of the skin under her fur slowly became crimson. There was a catch in Yama's voice as she replied, "You know your father and the others did everything they could to reinforce the homes. We are lucky that our home is in the trunk, not in the branches. Those families had to leave their homes behind to get closer to the tree's core to ride out the storm."

"Ok then... if this is the safest place, why did Yapa and the others leave? What'd they think they would find elsewhere?" Stella replied.

"None of us knew the storm would hit so soon, Stella. Their expedition was to gather more supplies. We didn't know they wouldn't make it back in time," Yama yelled to be heard over the growing noises of the storm.

"But where do you think he found shelter?" Ebert asked. He sobbed and his small body shook as he tried to speak. Stella fell silent. Her mother dropped her head and turned her attention back to Ebert. They had forgotten he was listening.

"Shhhhh. It's okay. Yapa is fine," Yama replied calmly, rocking Ebert to soothe him. She turned to Stella and leaned into her, her lips at Stella's ear, "*Enough*, Stella."

It was Stella's cheeks that burned now. She lowered her chin and closed her eyes. A deep, low growl echoed around her, and a chill caught in her bones, making her tremble. No storm had ever sounded like this before. A screech pierced the air, and Stella pressed her hands hard to her ears. All around her the tree responded to the storm. It sounded like it was alive, like it was one of them. It groaned and creaked as it fought the storm.

Then it suddenly shuddered. A quake rippled through its core.

Stella threw open her eyes. Water was gushing into the hollow of the tree. Limbs had been ripped from the tree's trunk and left behind holes exposing the terror of the storm. Water poured in the holes and flooded the bottom on the tree's hollow. The huge, arched doors that stood as the tree's entry where covered in a matter of moments. The water rose quickly and violently.

"Run… get higher… run… climb," a voice yelled from somewhere in the dark tree.

Stella and her mother jumped to their feet, her mother swung Ebert on her back. They staggered to join the other Trebors running and climbing towards the tree's inner core. Hundreds of Trebors scrambled up the core's central stairway, winding, winding, higher and higher. Those that couldn't climb were pulled to higher places by the chain of Trebors. Teams worked together to make sure the children were as high as they could go, giving them the chance to squeeze into the places in the core that only the smallest could possibly manage to fit in. Stella and her mother hurried to put Ebert into one of these nooks. He looked safe there, in one of the tree's most secure crevices. The adults and older children hung close by, tying themselves to parts of the tree attached to the core, digging their claws into the bark as deeply as they could. There was nowhere left to go now. They were as high as possible inside the tree. It was only a matter of time before the water would rise to meet them there. No one screamed. No one spoke. It was up to the tree now to keep them alive.

The tree groaned and screeched. Rain pounded the sides of the tree, thunder echoed along the inside walls. And then, just when Stella felt she couldn't withstand the tormenting noise any longer, it faded away. She relaxed her shoulders and smiled. But her relief was cut short as, to her horror, it was replaced by a torrent of harsh, crackling sound. It was even louder and more terrifying than the heavy rains. Explosions filled the air. Stella's ears rang. The tree shook as the giant booms filled the space where they all hid. It wasn't just Stella that shook, the other Trebors were all shaking as she was. Even her mother, a few inches from her, couldn't still her body. The sight scared Stella as much as the monstrous sounds around her. No Trebor was strong enough to stop it, even the elders were helpless, the torment of the storm was too great. Stella pressed herself closer to the tree wall and once again squeezed her eyes shut.

CHAPTER 2

Disoriented and exhausted, Stella could not tell how long she had been clinging to the inside of the tree. The sad and withdrawn look on her fellow Trebor's faces told her that she was not the only one losing hope.

And then, pirouetting through the tree, a small voice began to sing.

The little voice tumbled out from a crevice in the tree like a small beacon to the other Trebors clinging nearby. The sound was sweet, perfect, and seemed to hold no fear. One by one other Trebors began to sing along. With each new voice, the sounds of the storm seemed to fall away. Stella joined the singing too, her voice trembled as her off-key notes drifted to meet the notes of the others. Ebert's voice rose from his small hiding place, shaky at first but stronger with each passing verse, and soon her mother's voice rang out as well, her tone clear and strong. The collective voices bounced throughout the tree. They all sang as one. As their voices grew louder Stella could hear less of the storm, and with each new voice the howling seemed to wane. The storm let off another loud clap, but the Trebors only sang louder. The lightning still flashed, but the tree did not shake. As they sang, the low grumbles of the storm faded further and further away. As quickly as the anger of the storm had descending on them, it stopped. A stillness sat in the air and all of the Trebors fell silent.

Stella held her breath and looked carefully around her for the reaction of the others, she was afraid to exhale in case the silence would be broken and the storm roar again. Her ears perked up, standing in perfect triangles on top of her head. The little voice began to sing again. All at once, with voices loud and triumphant, every Trebor joined in. Stella pulled in her claws to release her grip and jumped to a platform below where she had been hanging, her wide feet smacked on the wood floor. Yama dropped down to join her. She sang loudly. Stella smiled and grabbed her mother's hand, weaving their long fingers together. Tears ran down Yama's face and Stella felt the salty taste of her own tears on her lips. Ebert crawled out of his hiding space and leapt into his mother's arms. Yama laughed and hugged them both tightly. Stella buried her head between her mother and her brother, taking a deep breath. They had made it… they were alive!

Time passed slowly as all of the Trebors cautiously came back to life. Families and friends scattered throughout the tree hugged, cried, and rejoiced at the passing of the storm. Stella's hands no longer trembled, and the shaking that had rattled her bones for so many hours also stopped. She wriggled her fingers, so the blood rushed back through her long, skinny hands, making her claws extend and her fur feel hot. She smoothed down the fur on her arms and brushed back the long, brown hair that had fallen into her eyes, tucking it behind her ears. She checked her knee and found a large bump with dried blood caked at its edges. She tried to brush the blood away, but it stung when she touched it and she pulled her hand away.

"Does it hurt?" Yama asked.

"No, it's fine, I'm fine," Stella replied.

"You could have been really hurt trying to move around during the storm by yourself."

"I was just trying to get to…" Stella began to reply, but Yama held up a tired hand and interrupted, "I don't want to hear 'I was just'," she said.

Stella nodded and avoided her mother's piercing, round eyes. She gritted her teeth. Ebert climbed closer to Stella and took her hand in his. He was still clutching his blanket with his other hand, but it was now a soggy mess. Stella took it from his hand and squeezed out the water. He smiled and took it back from her. His little ears perked up and a small smile pulled at the corner of his mouth, setting his small, button sized nose twitching. Stella tried to smile at her mother.

"Ok, sorry," Stella said.

Seeming satisfied with Stella's response, Yama squeezed her children to her again, giving them a long, hard hug before saying, "I need to find the other elders now and figure out what the plan is. Stella, look after Ebert."

"But don't you want to check our home first, Yama? We climbed away so quickly; shouldn't we make sure the water did not rise to its level?" Stella asked.

"You can go and check. Take your brother with you. I am more concerned with the homes built away from the core. I'm worried others have lost everything," Yama said. She started to climb towards a group of adults gathering on a landing nearby. Stella watched her mother climb away and shook her head.

The low hum of the Trebors' voices filled the vast, open hollow in the core of the tree. Trebors everywhere were taking stock of the damage left by the storm. Stretching thousands of feet above and below them the inside of the tree, her home, bore the signs of the storm's terror. Stella put her face in her hands and thought again of the day before. She had taken for granted the mighty doors that closed off the giant opening at the base of the tree. Everyday those doors were swung open and the sun jumped off their ornate carvings. Stella had often stood in front of them wondering how many Trebors it must have taken to create such beautiful, massive doors. She felt grateful for their strength that held off the worst of the storm. From those doors, she had always felt so small as she looked up at the massive inside hollow of the tree that stretched beyond her sight to the highest point of the tree's reach. The rumors of old suggested the tree was born of a match between the ancient sequoia and maple trees. No living Trebor had seen the days when the sequoia and maple trees populated the forests, but the elders told stories past down from generation to generation about these past trees. According to legend, the trunk of the great tree bore the breadth and might of the sequoia, while the branches and leaves reflected the grace of the maple tree. There was no other tree like their home in all of the lands of Bori or beyond.

The hollow inside the tree was walled by the tree's strong, smooth wood, its outer rings. The walls were thick enough for homes to be burrowed safely within them, a vertical city of homes. Giant, round openings pocked the inside of the tree's walls leading to tunnels that were the inside of the tree's branches. Small storage ran the length of these tunnels, stretching the Trebors' inside city to the tree's widest points. The core of the tree always shone with peaceful colors and warmth danced on its walls. In the center of the hollow, the inner most rings of the tree were built into a spiral staircase that twisted its way to the highest points of the tree. And somehow it had all survived.

Stella opened her eyes quickly to look again at the stairway. It was badly mangled at the bottom but remained mostly intact as it wound its way upward. Water pooled on some of the lower level landings that jutted out from homes in the tree's thick walls. The landings, which looked like shelf mushrooms climbing up the inside of the tree, were not damaged badly and Stella felt relieved. The cave-like homes burrowing into the tree walls were littered with food, furniture, clothes and treasure. Lifetimes' worth of family belongings were strewn everywhere. Many struggled through tears as they peered into their home. They had sad expressions that clung to their open, round faces.

"Come on Ebert, let's look for ourselves," Stella said.

Stella and Ebert carefully descended towards their home. The water below them was receding quickly, but the inside of the tree was still damp and chilly. Under Stella's hand, the usually warm bark of the tree felt slick and cold. As they climbed down, shadows fell over the landings, giving them only a dim light to illuminate their way. The meager light came from streams of sun piercing through gaps in the tree's wall. Great holes littered the walls of the inside of the tree where branches had been ripped from the trunk. So many crops and supplies had been nestled down the long tunnels of the branches. But now they were gone. Entire harvests had vanished, blown into the vortex of the storm. Stella stopped climbing and stared at a hole a few feet to her right. She fought back anger as she scurried towards the opening.

"I thought we're going home," Ebert said.

"Look," Stella pointed to the hole. "The branch is gone. It's just a window to outside now. I want to see. I want to know what it looks like out there."

"But Yama wouldn't like that. Shouldn't we go home and wait for the elders to tell us what to do?" Ebert rubbed his bright, blue eyes, they were red ringed and tired. Stella patted the damp fur on Ebert's shoulder, gave it a squeeze, smiled at him, and waved for him to follow her. Ebert's ears and nose twitched quickly. He climbed after his sister.

"STELLA!"

As Stella and Ebert reached the opening, Stella's best friend Snu swung through the air. He landed easily beside Stella, catching the bark with his claws. As he landed, the grey streaks in his light brown fur shimmered and his spiked hair bounced. "That was crazy! I thought we were goners for sure!" he exclaimed. Snu punched Stella on the arm and grinned. His wide smile made his green eyes crinkle at the edges; the grey patch that surrounded his left eye made it sparkle in contrast.

"How can you joke?" Stella demanded.

Snu's face grew serious. He lifted his left shoulder. "Sorry, I was just, I don't know, trying to lighten things."

Stella huffed.

"Ebert and I are going to take a look outside. I want to see what happened out there. Wait—Ebert? EBERT?"

Ebert had already climbed ahead of them. He slid his small body through one of the new holes created by the storm. His clawed feet dug deep into the bark as he steadied himself to shimmy through the space.

"Ugh," Stella groaned and raced to the hole as Ebert disappeared. She stuck her head through the hole to see where Ebert had gone. He was hanging onto the rough bark outside. The look Stella saw on his face scared her, his wide eyes were glazed over with fear and sadness. She followed his stare.

She gasped.

Everything in Bori was destroyed. The forest floor was black and crackling. Smoke rose from the smoldering earth like snakes through the air. Pools of water gathered in great holes throughout the forest floor. A thin black film lay on top of the pools, catching the sun and sending an ugly glare off the surfaces. The few standing trees had no branches and looked like lone soldiers on a battlefield. Stella could not see beyond the hills to Mt. Bor because of the haze that filled the sky. The smoke clung to the air all around them. The sour stench of the air burnt the inside of her nose and the smoke stung her eyes. Ebert remained frozen, his eyes fixed ahead, his mouth hanging low.

"We should go back in," she said.

"Where's Yapa?" he asked in a whisper.

"He's fine, he'll be back soon, he has to be," Stella mumbled. She grabbed Ebert's arm and yanked him through the hole and back into the tree.

Throughout the grand, central hollow of the tree, the other Trebors were busy greeting one another and celebrating their survival. They moved quickly from home to home, up and down the twisting staircase. A happy buzz filled the space.

"They haven't seen yet. They don't know," Ebert muttered.

"I know," Stella sighed. "They haven't even looked."

"But the tree did save us, Stella. Why wasn't Yapa here where we were safe?" Ebert asked.

"I wish I knew," Stella huffed.

"What'd you see?" Snu interrupted, his eyes creasing at the edges.

Stella pulled Snu by the arms and dragged him to the hole. She grabbed his shoulder, pushing him against the opening. His plump body tightened and then deflated as she held his shoulder. Snu turned, wide-eyed, and looked at her, "Oh…" was all he could say.

The three climbed wordlessly to where Yama was standing with the other elders. They were an impressive group of Trebors. Their round, smooth faces, huge, wide set eyes and lopsided nostrils sitting on their button sized noses all mirrored each other in intensity. Their furrowed brows made the gentle, pink skin wrinkle under the light fur that covered their faces. Their ears did not move, but stood in formation like two mountain peaks on top of their heads. Their noses twitched so quickly they gave away the grave nature of the conversation. The dark brown streak that ran down Yama's back stood on end and Stella reflectively flattened the brown, speckled fur on her arm. She wished she had the same light brown fur with the single streak of dark that made her mother so stunning, but instead she looked like her father. They were unique he used to tell Stella, and although she knew it gave them a very special bond, it did little to make her feel better. Both she and Yapa had bright, white fur lining their chests while the rest of the Trebors' bodies covered in light brown fur. They all had their own hair colors and markings on their fur, but other than Yapa, no other Trebor had such a distinct difference like Stella's fronted, white streak. It was Ebert that looked most like their mother. His blue eyes, blond hair, and even colored, light brown fur were a perfect match. At least she too had Yama's long blond hair that spiked from her forehead until it fell flat and smooth to her shoulders. She was also just as strong and fit as her, if not more.

"Yama, Yama…" Stella got hold of her mother's shirt and gently tugged.

"Not now, Stella. We are talking about how to proceed, what to do next. Just watch Ebert and stay inside."

"But you haven't seen. Everything's gone," Stella insisted.

"I know. The others told me," Yama replied.

"But you haven't seen. Don't you want to see with your own eyes?"

"I trust the report from the others. For now, I'm more interested in making sure everyone is safe and cared for before nightfall. Now, please take your brother. Go. Be useful and leave us to figure out what needs to be done," Yama responded.

Stella threw her arms up and let them drop to her side. Yama ignored her dramatic gesture and turned back to the group.

"What's most important is that we stick together," Stella overheard Elder Malc saying. "I believe we should call for a tribe curfew. Night is almost upon us and we are safest together here, inside the tree. All Trebors should remain here until morning breaks." Elder Malc's voice carried through the passage as Stella walked away.

"Trapped again, useless…" she muttered under her breath.

CHAPTER 3

Stella woke abruptly. She sat up to shake the dark dream from her thoughts. The terror of the storm still clung to the edges of her mind. She wrapped her arms across her chest and rubbed them vigorously. The movement did little to stop her trembling. Her mind raced as the dread from the day before slowly seeped back into her awakening world. The night had not numbed the reality of the storm's damage. The forest had been scorched and she couldn't fathom how close the fire had been to their home before the rains took over. *How had the tree not caught fire? How were they still alive?* The worst part was that her father's face kept flashing into her vision, anguish and despair clung to his face.

Ebert and Yama were curled up together on a blanket nearby, sleeping soundly. Although Ebert was already seven, he still at times seemed so much smaller, and seeing him curled up with Yama reminded Stella how little he still was. For a moment, she wished she could curl up with them, too; but she had other plans. First, though, she was hungry. Before the family went to sleep the night before, they had turned the table back on its feet and gathered any unspoiled food. On the table sat a dense loaf of kasha bread topped with seeds and a basket of yaza fruit. Stella's stomach growled. She crept over to the food and ripped off a piece of kasha. It was stale and stuck to the roof of her mouth as she chewed. She grabbed a long, green yaza fruit and snapped it in half. The inside was green, firm and crisp, and a few bites quickly made up for the dryness of the kasha bread. The food did not settle the tightness in her stomach, but the grumbling stopped. When she was done, she wiped her hands against her pale brown jumper and then pulled her hair into a knot at the back of her head.

Stella tiptoed onto the landing that projected out from her home. As she peered into the cavernous space of the tree's core, she saw little movement and heard only the sounds of snoring. With their round noses and nostrils that jutted up and down each of a different size, when Trebors slept it sounded like a chorus of bullfrogs. This morning was no exception. Even her own mother, just a few feet away, honked and whistled. The noise annoyed Stella; she was irritated that they all slept while her father was still unaccounted for. The light that poured like spotlights through the holes in the tree highlighted the mess left by the storm, further enraging her. Stella rubbed the fingers on her right hand back and forth on her thumb as she peered into their broken lives. There was so much work to be done, so much healing to take place. But she didn't care about that: she had to form her own plan and find her father. Seeing that the section of the circular stairs in front of their landing was broken, Stella climbed along the tree's walls towards one of the holes. She hadn't seen enough yesterday when Ebert climbed out. She wanted to understand for herself the damage the storm had left in its wake. Surely, the curfew no longer applied as it was technically sunrise.

Outside the tree, Stella rested on a knobby bump on the bark. She tented her hand over her eyes to see past the sun's bright streams. A tickle caught in her throat and made her cough; smoke lingered on the heavy air. Below her, the clearing that surrounded the tree looked charred; the soft green grass and springy moss that served as a center of the Trebors' lives had been replaced by a blanket of black with small, gray mounds of soot that still glowed slightly red as they burned. At the edge of the clearing, the forest brambles were flattened and also black; bare branches lay across forest paths. Huge trees now hugged the earth, their roots upended, and their branches stripped of leaves. A black film that had settled on the pools of water also dripped from the overturned trees. It slid like molasses from the trees and ran into the pools of water.

From her perch high above the lands of Bori Stella could also see that the crop fields had been completely decimated. The quinold trees were flattened; the giant gourds that grew from their branches until they touched the ground were gone. Even the most vibrant red and purple quinolds were out of sight, destroyed. She hoped that crops like the flanuts and pink beans that grew low to the ground on vines might have survived. But she knew, without even seeing it, that their staple fields, the kasha grain fields, had not stood a chance, and she hoped that the tree's storage crevices were full.

In the distance, Mt. Bor was still covered in low hanging clouds and a dark haze. Behind the mountain, the clouds and sky were black as night, with streaks of red like flames that licked at the air as they burned. She tried to see the rugged path that encircled the mountain, winding its way up and over the great Bor. For years she had watched this path from the tree, a path she had never walked, yet had always wanted to. She wondered again what was on the other side: only a few Trebors had been over the mountain and they never spoke of it. The same black film that dripped from the carnage around the tree also streamed down the mountainside. She shuddered. There were rumors of evil that lurked near the mountain, but Stella knew they were stories parents told to keep the young Trebors close to the tree. She had even heard whispers of lost tribes of Trebors. This rumor went so far as to say that the elders all took oaths to never speak of them. The stories always felt foolish to Stella, but now she felt a deepened pang of worry for Yapa.

She coughed again to clear her throat, but the singed air scraped the top of her throat. Then an explosive hacking racked her whole body, making her head shake and jerk.

"There she is!" It was Ebert's voice.

As Stella struggled to still her cough, she caught sight of the even toned fur on Ebert's back as he climbed towards her. Just like the rest of the Trebors, Ebert's had short, stubby legs that were often slow to maneuver when he climbed. Snu's head appeared next through the haze, with his unmistakable spikey brown hair.

"What are you doing?" Stella said through her coughing.

Ebert climbed over and onto the bump where Stella sat; he threaded his arm through hers. Snu climbed alongside, his usually extended stomach squished flat against the tree as he climbed.

"Us? What are we doing here? We came to find you!" Snu said.

"I woke up and you weren't there. I was scared," Ebert added.

Snu banged Stella on the back, hard. Her coughing stopped and she exhaled slowly, her nose stinging.

"He crept into my home and woke me up to find you. I knew you'd be out here."

"How could you know that?" Stella demanded.

"Because you never listen. You always find a way to bend the rules and do things yourself," Snu said.

Stella rolled her eyes. She said, "Did you ever think that maybe I wanted to be alone? Maybe I don't need you following me."

"Ebert was worried. I said I'd help. So, can you just come back in and wait for direction from the elders?" Snu implored.

"Ebert, you don't have to worry about me I am... Ebert? *Ebert?*"

Above Stella and Snu, Ebert's big, flat feet disappeared into the haze.

"Ebert! stop!" Stella yelled. "I can barely see you through this air. It's not safe to go any higher. Get back down here." But the thick air swallowed her words. Ebert faded out of sight.

Stella glanced at Snu. They rushed towards the crown of the tree.

"You should have just sent him back home to Yama. Why would you bring him out here?" Stella snarled. Snu did not reply.

As they climbed higher and higher the burning in Stella's nose began to subside. Her watering eyes cleared. Large sections of bark had been ripped from the trunk and while the branches were intact, no leaves remained. Yet the tree was still strong. Stella and Snu climbed easily, spreading their long fingers and digging in with their claws.

"Stop, Ebert! Wait. We are coming—stop climbing," Stella yelled.

Ebert stopped and looked down at Stella and Snu. His nose twitched.

"Look! Look!" Ebert yelled, pointing to the top of the tree. Stella peered up. The haze that hung in the air above was glowing. She turned to Snu, but he was already racing towards the crown of the tree. Stella and Ebert followed.

At the top, they could see more clearly. The tree cast a green light into the haze below. It shone. The tree bark glowed with a green aura. The strange hue was brightest at the top of the tree, but as the three Trebors glanced down they could see that the entire tree was bathed in this color.

"It's like it's alive," Ebert whispered.

Stella squeezed her eyes shut. When she opened them again, the weird color remained the same. She lay both hands flat on the bark. "It's warm. The bark is warm." She pressed her face against the tree; the warmth tingled her checks and she laughed.

Snu and Ebert did the same and soon they were all laughing. They laughed for a long time, becoming giddier as each moment passed.

"You know," Snu said through gasps as he laughed, "I could swear there are leaves popping out of that branch."

Stella rubbed her eyes. She looked to where Snu was pointing. "That's not a leaf. There is no way. I think this strange air is making us see things," she said.

Ebert climbed along the branch and grasped a tiny, green bud. He pulled hard and tumbled back as a fist full of bright green leaves tore from the branch.

"See… it was a leaf," Snu yelled. "The tree must be growing in super speed."

"It's healing itself right in front of us!" Stella shouted back.

Ebert laughed again and laid flat across the branch on his back; he held the leaves high above his head. He rolled from side to side scratching his back and swinging his legs around. Stella chuckled at the sight of Ebert's short and stubby legs bent towards the sky, flinging around.

"The tree is doing all of the work! The tree is fixing itself!" Ebert sang as he wriggled.

"He's right. If the tree is really healing itself, and at such a great speed, there will be time for the elders to send out a search team for our fathers and the others," Snu said.

"Yes! We have to tell the elders at once. There should be enough hands for the search team to form quickly if there is less work to do here," Stella said.

Wasting no time, they climbed down the tree. At the base of the tree, where the green clearing had been the morning before, most of the Trebors wandered over the now blackened earth. The air at the bottom was still thick with ash and the Trebors snorted and coughed, a sound that was loud and jarring to Stella's ears. The smallest Trebors whimpered at their parent's feet, still half-asleep and scared by the destruction around them. Other Trebors comforted the young ones and offered support to others. With no time to spare, Stella, Snu, and Ebert pushed through the crowd until they spotted Yama with Snu's mother. They stood somberly with the elders at the front of the crowd. Ebert ran to them. Stella and Snu followed quickly.

"Look at the tree, Yama!" Ebert exclaimed.

"Quiet, child. Elder Malc is about to speak."

"But he needs to know what we found," Stella said; but all around her the crowd had grown silent.

"My fellow Trebors. We must not be afraid by what we see but rejoice in our safety. Against all odds, the tree has saved us. Although difficult work now looms ahead of us, we must be as strong as this faithful tree that protected us. Together we will rebuild."

"Elder Malc, Elder Malc! We have discovered something important. It is good news…" Stella blurted out.

"Child. There is a time to speak and this is not it," Elder Malc said.

Yama glared at Stella, sending her an angry, silencing look. Stella ignored the rebuke and instead took a step forward.

"What I have to say is important. It's about the tree."

"Stella, stop," Yama warned. She grabbed Stella by the back of her arm. Stella struggled to pull away, but her mother's grasp was firm and unyielding. Yama dragged her out of the crowd.

"Now you will not be disrespectful anymore. Do not address Elder Malc. Do not try to interfere with the grown-ups. It is not your place. It is your place to follow the rules. Do as you're told and help us rebuild. That's it!"

"But, Yama. I was only trying to…"

"Enough. Stay here. When we have figured out how to proceed, you will be given a job. Until then, keep your mouth shut and stay out of the way." Yama turned abruptly and stormed back into the group.

Stella slid to the ground but jumped up quickly as it was hot. A cloud of ash covered her. She slapped angrily at her clothes trying to brush off the ash. Her nose burned again, and she coughed hard. "They never listen," she muttered under her breath.

She watched as the Trebors stood in silence, huddled together, hands clasped with one another and arms around shoulders. They listened to Elder Malc, her mother, and the other elders. Stella could not hear their words, but she could tell from the way the other Trebors stood still and very erect that the instructions were to be strong and band together. The message was always the same. Stay close to the tree. Work together. She had heard it enough and now she yearned for something different. This time she wanted to hear that they were jumping into action and sending a team to find her father. If he were there, he would not sit still and wait. Yapa would demand action, or at the very least, let her speak. His fellow elders always listened to him. They said he had seen things that gave him great insight. Stella wondered if maybe this was why he had led the scouting trip that took him away from the tree during the storm.

The brush nearby bristled and Stella jumped. She bent down to look into the thick, burnt bushes and tangled branches, but saw nothing. She shrugged and stood up.

"You okay?" Snu appeared by Stella's side.

"They are missing it all. They're so busy planning, but the tree is already doing the work. If only they would listen. If only they would stop and look! Why do they never listen?"

"I don't know, but I do know they didn't talk once about our fathers. I listened to old Malc's stupid speech. It was all about rebuilding, banding together, no talk of sending a search party. In fact, he announced that we were all to stay close to the tree. The elders don't want us leaving the safety of our home and each other.

You were right about following the code of togetherness instead of splitting up."

"Our mothers didn't speak up, no doubt."

"Nope."

Stella dropped her voice until it was almost a whisper, "What if the rumors of some sort of evil living under Mt. Bor are true? What if our fathers are facing more danger than what the storm caused?"

"Come on, Stel, you don't believe that," Snu replied. "Those are just tales, as crazy as the talk that there is another tribe of Trebors. You know that's not true."

"Then why don't they ever let us go to the mountain? And why now do we have to stay by the tree?" Stella replied.

"Because we don't know what damage the storm left. It could be treacherous beyond our home," Snu answered.

Stella shook her jumper urgently and banged on her pants one more time so that soot leapt from her clothes. She turned to Snu. "I'm going," she said.

"Where?" Snu asked

"To find our fathers!"

"No, you are not. We have to wait. We'd have more luck finding them and helping them if we have more Trebors with us."

"No, I can't wait. I'm tired of following the code. All of the rules feel like a brick wall closing me in. Stay close to the tree, don't go out alone, work as a team…"

"No, Stel. We wait."

"You can wait. I'm not. I don't need the tribe to do this."

Snu grew quiet and stared into the burnt forest. He reached out his hand and rubbed it along a branch that was tangled in the brush. The black slime slid between his fingers and tangled in his fur.

"Look," he said holding his slime-covered hand towards Stella. "We don't know what kind of a storm this was and what it has left behind. The only thing left living is the tree. Why leave it? It's our safety."

"We leave it because our fathers aren't here."

"But what good are we to them alone?"

"I don't know, but I know that I'm going to try. I can't just stay here and wait. I'm going to prove to myself and everyone else that I can do so much more than they ever let me."

Snu nodded. He rubbed his hands together to remove the soot. Stella reached over to pull pieces of the sticky substance from his fur.

"I'll go with you," Snu said.

"No, I don't want you to," Stella insisted.

"It's not always just about what you want. I'm not letting you do this alone."

"I can do it. You stay with our mothers. Keep Ebert out of harm's way or trouble," Stella said.

"I'm only saying this one more time. You can't do it alone. I won't let you."

"You sound as bad as them, why don't you believe in me?"

"That's not it. I believe in you. I just want to come, okay? That's all. I want to help, too!"

Stella kicked the ash on the forest floor with her foot and shifted her weight back and forth. "Fine," she finally replied.

CHAPTER 4

"Do you have everything?" Stella whispered to Snu as she quietly rummaged through her own pack to make sure she hadn't forgotten anything.

It was night, and she felt a chill in the air. Darkness engulfed the clearing where they stood. The air smelled like the stale logs of their cooking fires that had burnt out and been left to turn to ash. Her nagging cough threatened to seize her again; the tickle that crept up her throat felt like little fingers dancing inside. Stella swallowed hard and exhaled. The grunts and snores of the Trebors asleep in the tree filled the air and she took courage that this chorus of noise would keep anyone from hearing them. Still, she was growing impatient to start their journey.

After having been dismissed by Yama and the other elders, Stella was more determined than ever to venture out on her own. She was irritated by Snu's insistence to join her but had come to accept that she had no choice in the matter. The two had spent the day planning their search. Their mothers had been so busy tending to the needs of the tribe that they didn't noticed Stella and Snu's absence. Not wanting to be caught, they had spent the day on the tree's top branches, watching as the tree forced tender buds and dancing leaves along its branches. The speed of the new growth energized Stella as she and Snu plotted their journey.

"I think I have everything. I even grabbed my father's guiding stone. I realized a few days ago that he did not take it with him, so I figured we might as well bring it," Snu replied.

"What color is it now?" Stella asked.

"Blue. Calm. I guess that's a good sign."

"Do you know what all of the colors mean? Otherwise it won't be of much use," Stella said.

"Yes. You don't?"

"I never paid attention to Yapa when we spoke of it."

"Well, I did, turns out that was a good thing."

Stella shook her head, "Yapa left his pouch. I saw it during the storm and now I realize I forgot to get it. I don't know what's in it, but it must be important enough as he usually always wears it."

"It's too late now, we can't go back in," Snu replied.

"You're right," Stella sighed.

Stella handed Snu a headlamp. "Anyway, put this on. I brought two," she said.

She secured hers on her own head. She pulled two glow rocks from her pack and put one in her lamp and one in Snu's. Along with being farmers, the Trebors were inventors and the discovery of the glow rocks had been recent and created great change for the tribe. She was glad now for this latest invention. She flicked on her lamp and took a look around to get her bearings. The wreckage in the forest ahead of them was dense and looked impassible. They had talked about how difficult it would be to trek through the tangled bushes and downed trees, but when Stella saw the extent of the damage, the path looked ominous. She took her first step into the wreckage.

"Stel," Snu's voice broke Stella's frozen stare. "Are you sure about this? We can wait for the tribe, wait for others."

Stella shook her head as a wave of fatigue rolled over her. They had been over the plan, over and over it. They needed to get to the other side of Mt. Bor. From the tree they would have caught sight of Yapa and the others if they were in Bor still, but they hadn't seen anything. This left only the possibility that they had traveled over the mountain and were stuck on the other side where the dark clouds still loomed. Stella had argued that if the tales were true and there was evil lurking under the mountain this could be why Yapa had not come home. Snu had fiercely disagreed and Stella finally gave in to the plan to go over Mr. Bor and search for her father and the others there, instead of believing old rumors.

"I have to do this," she said, and walked towards the shadowy forest.

The noise of the Trebor's snoring soon faded into the distance and an eerie quiet settled around them. Stella and Snu pushed through the thicket and climbed over the trees and branches that littered the forest floor. As they moved through the forest, they had to crawl through openings among the debris to find clearer paths. Each step was slow and arduous as black film dripped from the branches and caught in their fur making them sticky and hot. Sharp thorns gripped their skin as they tried to maneuver through tight spaces, causing them to stop every few steps. Their progress was painfully gradual and fraught with difficulty. Even when they came to a place where the forest gave way to a wider space, pools of water that filled cavernous holes hindered their way. Upturned trees and bushes had created the holes where they were pulled from their roots, and there was no way of knowing how deep they ran. They had to travel in wide loops around these crater pools while avoiding ground that still smoldered and burned. Snu huffed and grunted giving away his doubt that they were doing the right thing. Stella ignored him and kept her eyes trained on the ground ahead, pushing them closer to the mountain.

"I'm not sure we are going to make it to Mt. Bor before daybreak," Snu finally said.

"We have to. The only way to get over the mountain without the others seeing us from the tree is to travel in the dark," Stella replied.

"I know, but this terrain is so much harder to traverse than we thought. Time is not working with us."

Stella ignored Snu and kept her head down as she chose every step with care. Eventually, they stopped at the edge of another enormous pool of water. Black film floated on the top and bubbled in places like a boiling pot of stew. Snu threw a rock into the pond and it landed on the black film. Slowly the strange substance engulfed it, sucking the rock under the water. Stella's eyes widened as she turned to Snu, "That could pull us under in seconds. I'm not sure we could even move in there if we fell."

"I still don't understand what that is or how it got here," Snu said.

"And there was so much rain and wind at the beginning of the storm, I don't know how everything burned," Stella said.

"You heard the storm change its moans in the middle right? I thought the rains, winds, and thunder were never going to end. But when they did, I heard noises I never had before!"

"Yes! It sounded like explosions."

"And the crackling and hissing… it was awful!"

"That must have been what caused the burning."

"Do you think fire came from the clouds? Do you think this black filth did, too?"

"I don't know, but I overheard the elders saying that they had never heard a storm like that before and never seen the black before."

"Remember those dark, heavy clouds that loomed behind the mountain? They were there for weeks. Then the storm came. I wonder if they brought the storm?"

Stella stopped and rubbed her feet, which were burning.

"I just hope wherever that storm came from, it never comes again," Stella said firmly. "You did fill the canisters with fresh water right?" She wiped her hands against her fur and reached for her canister.

"Of course I did," Snu said, rolling his eyes. "It's a good thing the spouts from the tree were not damaged or we would be in trouble."

"That's another thing that's making me scared for our fathers," Stella sighed. "If the only fresh water our tribe could find came directly from the tree, what are our fathers doing?"

Snu's face fell flat.

"I'm sure they found water," Snu murmured.

"You don't know that. If they are hurt or trapped or…" Stella let her voice trail off.

"Stop, Stella. That doesn't help either of us," Snu snapped. Snu shook his head as if shaking off questions he didn't want to answer. "We've been through this, there is nothing evil at or under Mr. Bor. Let it go."

Stella leaned over the edge of the pool and stared at her reflection in a small clear patch of water. She fought back tears. She looked tired and pale in the murky water. Her mind swirled with tormented thoughts of her father, images she tried to chase away. The noises in the forest around her sounded strange and made her jumpy; the snapping, crackling, and popping filled her ears. Her eyes darted towards the forest and then back to the water. Suddenly, a flash reflected off the water. The thick brush next to her rustled. Stella jumped and grabbed Snu's arm. She pulled him roughly towards her. Her heart beat so quickly she could barely catch her breath. The fur on the back of her neck stood at attention.

"Did you see that?" she asked.

"No. What? Where?"

"I saw… I don't know what, and then a noise from that upturned tree!"

"A new noise? Which tree?"

"Over there." Stella pointed to the base of a mangled tree. The roots were a tangled mess, angry from being torn from the ground they now hovered over. The black film dripped off the spindly roots, and ash gathered in the dense mud beneath the tree. Stella's knees wobbled. She spread her arms to steady herself. She took a step closer and shone her light into the roots. There… a rustling. Stella froze. Her heart throbbed at the back of her throat. She swallowed. Snu's breath quickened beside her.

"Did you hear that?" Stella whispered.

Suddenly a black streak flew towards Stella.

Whack!

It grabbed her face and clung to both side of her cheeks. The jolt knocked her to the ground.

"Help!" Stella grabbed at her face and pulled. The creature was slimy and scaly.

"Snu – do something!"

Snu's hands were quickly next to hers. Both of them clawed and pulled, trying to free her. Each time they tugged it felt like the skin on Stella's face would rip off. It felt like hundreds of tiny suction cups were pulling at her skin. Her cheeks stretched until tears sprang from her eyes.

"Stop – stop! It's so painful. What is it? Can you see what it is?"

"It's some sort of animal, I think. I've never seen it before. It's the color of your skin and has hundreds of legs and tiny little feet," Snu yelled.

"Do something! Help me," Stella screamed.

"I'm trying! Its feet are grabbing your face like suction cups. Pulling is just making them tighten." Snu said as he panted for breath. He let go.

Stella lay very still, her back pressed against the upturned roots. Pained seared through her face. She took a deep breath and exhaled. When she did it again, her cheeks loosened, and the pain slowed. She breathed deeply again. In and out, looser; in and out, looser.

"What's happening?" Snu yelled.

Stella felt her heart speed up. The creature's feet began pulling again.

"Be quiet!" She snarled at Snu.

Stella breathed again: in and out. In and out. Slowly she felt the feet release; the tension on her face eased. She closed her eyes and concentrated on being calm. Soon she felt something cold and smooth drop across her whole face and slide off to the side. She jumped up and spun around to shine her headlamp where she had been sitting. There in the spotlight a creature stared at her, the color of its skin changing from a pinkish hue that resembled the skin under her fur, to a black sheen that picked up the color of the scorched earth where it now stood. It was much smaller than Stella and low to the ground, but long, so long. It had hundreds of tiny legs that shivered in place along its sleek body. Its tail stood upright and curled at the end. As Stella put her arms in front of her and steadied her footing, Snu came alongside her and did the same. They stood still.

There was a high-pitched hiss and the creature straightened its head. "I do apologiiiiiiize," it said.

The fur on the back of Stella's neck rose. Snu grabbed her forearm and gripped tightly. Stella's jaw dropped. Snu let go of her arm and adjusted his headlamp. He leaned in closer to examine the strange creature. The creature cocked its giant, round head. It had huge, red, bulging eyes, but no nose. Spikes rose from its scaly skin, making a ring around its face.

"Who… what are you?" Stella whispered.

The creature raised the front of its body with its long arms. Its whole body stretched to the size and length of the centipedes they knew from the forest, but it only had the vague look of the creatures they knew. Its head hovered over its arms, jutting straight out of its tube-like body, upright and alert. Its eyes glowed.

"As I said, I do apologiiiiiize. When I am afraid, I lose control of my fingers. I only meant to scare you away when I jumped. But I landed most unfortunately on your face… and then my feet… hisssssss. You felt it. They just took over."

Stella stared at the creature in silence. Its scales reflected the light from her headlamp and shimmered. Its red eyes blazed. A cold chill tickled the tips of Stella's fingers. Her spine felt as stiff as a rod.

"I'm a malped," the creature continued. I was trapped in the rains of the storm." It let out a loud hiss as it spoke. "I had no control; I was pulled through the rapids, tumbling for hours. When I finally stopped, I found myself here in this strange forest."

Stella looked at Snu and raised an eyebrow. A slow grin spread across the creature's face, revealing a wide mouth, with no teeth.

"Why believe you?" Snu asked.

"Why would I lie to you? I am *alone* in the dark of niiiiight," it hissed.

"You almost ripped the skin off my face. How can you say you had no control?" Stella yelled back, finally finding her voice.

"I would not like to rip your skin," it replied.

"I spent the day looking for other malpeds," it continued. "I found none. I had just settled into the roots of that dead tree to find protection for the night when your lights startled me. I am sorry. I was scaaaaared."

Still Stella did not reply. Snu remained silent as well.

"I just want to get home. I mean no harm," the malped pleaded. The shivering in its legs stopped all at once and it again cocked its head to look at them. The tiny spikes around its eyes reflected the red of its eyes. Suddenly, Stella found it hard to look away.

Snu grabbed Stella's arm. He turned her to look at him, "Walk away," he warned.

Stella took a step back as Snu pulled at her arm. The tiny legs on the malped began to move in rhythm up and down its long body, but it did not move towards them. Stella and Snu took another step backward and slowly turned to walk away. Over her shoulder, Stella said, "Good luck, malped. We hope you find your home soon."

"Thank youuuuuu," it replied. Its voice now sounded quiet, stranded, and sad.

Stella stopped.

"No," Snu whispered harshly. "Do not feel sorry for that creature. We don't know what it really is!"

"But it didn't really hurt me," Stella replied. "And it's obviously lost out here without its other malpeds. How can we just leave it?"

"Something doesn't feel right, Stel. And besides, helping this *thing* is not our journey. We need to keep moving to get to our fathers."

"How can you say it doesn't feel right? Nothing feels right. I can't trust any of this. The forest around us is dead, but this creature survived. To me, that's the only good thing I've seen since we left home."

"That's my point! How could it have survived when nothing else did? It's not right."

"Maybe it's special. Maybe it can help us find our fathers."

"Or maybe not… and it will distract us and bring us harm. We don't know and it's not worth the risk."

Stella curled her hands into a ball of worry.

"Ok. Maybe you are right. Besides, we need to pick up our pace if we want to get over the mountain before daybreak. Every minute we lose here is a minute we're not helping our fathers."

Stella furrowed her brow and turned back to the malped. "We are sorry for your struggles, malped. But we have to be back on our journey now. We wish you well." With that, she returned to the path, and Snu followed.

"Good," Snu said under his breath as they made their way forward.

"The mountain…hisssss. The mountain… hisss…."

Stella's skin prickled. When she looked up, the malped stood in the path in front of them, its tiny legs again shivering. She shook off the matching shiver that ran down her spine.

CHAPTER 5

"I would like to travel with you over the mountain. I can help with your journeeeeeey," the malped said.

"How did you get in front of us?" Snu hissed in response.

The shivering in the malped's legs stopped, and it turned its head again to the side and froze. Stella watched the malped and then looked sideways at Snu, whose eyes were now slits disappearing into his fur.

"I don't think we really have a choice right now," she said.

She swallowed hard and took a few deliberate steps towards the malped. Her heart raced. Just as she was about to reach the creature, it moved. Smoothly, it slid to the side of the path next to her and followed her without making a sound. Stella worked to calm her nerves and force her feet to take one step in front of the other. Snu grumbled from behind and stomped his foot. She turned and glared at him.

"Do you see another choice?" she demanded.

"There is always another choice!" Snu shot back.

"But it's going to follow anyway, and I think it could help. Look at it Snu, it's so small and it needs help," Stella replied.

"It hurt you," Snu yelled.

"I'm fine. Let's just go, we're wasting time," Stella answered, and with that she moved forward. Snu reluctantly followed.

The group travelled through the dead forest without speaking; the scorched brush crackled around them and the smell of damp, rotting leaves mingled with a strange scent that still hung in the air. With each hour, they became increasingly more agile at maneuvering through the chaos that spread before them. They settled into a rhythm on the uneven, harsh paths they forged through the forest. Snu did not speak to Stella and she didn't try to engage him. Though she was moving faster, Stella grew increasingly weary. The malped had not spoken again either, it just moved slowly with them. Its eyes fixated on the terrain ahead, its skin changing colors in unison with the surroundings. One moment it was as black as the charred earth. The next, it was the gray of smoldering soot. When Stella turned her light to look at the malped, it reflected back the brightness, although the color was indistinguishable. She began to wonder if she was too tired to continue. The noise in the forest unsettled Stella and she could swear that she heard more footsteps in the forest behind her, but every time she turned there was nothing.

After hours of walking, Stella suggested a break. She hoped that a rest and some water might calm her nerves and soothe her raw senses. They found a dry place to rest on the forest floor, where both Snu and Stella collapsed, exhausted. The malped curled into a tight ball nearby and fell asleep, making a high-pitched purring noise that echoed in the small space that surrounded them. Snu shook his head and glanced at Stella.

"I think we should sneak off now while it's sleeping. You have to trust me. I feel it. Something's not right. And look at my father's guiding stone... it's black."

Stella took the stone from Snu and rubbed her thumb over its smooth surface. She peered closely at how dark the stone had become and felt a chill come over her.

"Doesn't black mean danger? When did it change colors?" she asked.

"I'm not sure exactly. I only noticed it an hour ago when I pulled it from my pocket to be sure we were on the right track."

"Why didn't you tell me then?"

"I didn't want that *thing* to hear me talking. I don't want it to know that I have something so valuable in my pocket."

"Do you think it's because the malped is with us?" Stella asked.

"I don't know for sure, but we can't ignore it," Snu replied.

"It could mean we are going the wrong way or maybe it senses that our fathers are in trouble and there's danger ahead."

"No, Stel. It's that thing," Snu replied, and pointed his finger at the malped. His claw thrust forward and retracted quickly.

Stella handed the stone back to Snu and opened her pack. She took out her water and took a long sip, offering some to Snu when she was done. He shook his head no as he glared at her. She wiped her lips with the back of her hand and glared back.

"Don't be naïve, Stella. Now's our chance to split ways. Let's take it," Snu growled.

"Fine. But just so I've said it: it doesn't feel right, leaving it here, alone. It has been fine, all these hours with us."

"It survived the worst storm we have ever known. It will be fine."

Stella gave up. She was too tired to keep arguing and she was anxious to ease the tension she felt.

She quietly got to her feet and Snu did the same. They tiptoed past the malped, carefully placing each foot as they moved. They were soon a few feet from the malped. They picked up their pace. Stella glanced over her shoulder as they hurried away. She startled as the malped suddenly opened its eyes and stared straight into Stella's. The gaze was piercing. Stella stopped walking.

"Hisssssssssss… is it time to go?" the malped asked.

Snu stopped in his tracks. He dropped his head and sighed. Stella shoved him in the back.

"Why don't you just go back!" she spat. "This isn't my fault."

Snu threw his arms up in the air and turned to face her.

"I never told you I needed you in the first place," Stella said, but a frantic scream interrupted her.

"Help!"

"What was that?" Stella asked. Her eyes widened as panic surged through her.

"The screaming is coming from over there…" he said, pointing to the burnt thrush ahead.

"*Help*!"

"That sounded like a Trebor. Hurry!" Stella yelled.

Stella and Snu sprinted through the forest, stumbling as they went. The malped raced ahead of them, as if flying along the forest floor. The screaming became louder and more panicked. They ran faster.

"*Ebert*!" Snu screamed as they got closer to the screaming. "Stella, it's Ebert... it's Ebert!"

Stella's ears began to ring as her heart thundered. Ebert's head bobbed in a pool of water ahead; thick black, slimy liquid dripped down his face. Stella tried to catch his eyes by waving her arms over her head.

"Snu, we have to get there now. He can't swim, and the black will pull him under!"

As soon as they got close enough to the enormous hole of water, Stella and Snu dropped to their knees. Ebert reached his hand to Stella and she grabbed it.

"I've got you," she said, but his hand slipped through hers. His head slid under the water and he struggled to bring it back to the surface. Ebert reached his hand to Stella. She grabbed his palm, but his hand slipped from hers. She clutched at his fingers as his chin slid into the black liquid. His blue eyes blinked at her, then he squeezed them shut. He took a sharp breath before his round nose was consumed by water and black film.

Stella screamed.

Snu dove into the water.

Everything went quiet.

"*Ebert*! *Snu*!" Stella hollered over and over.

She stood and wailed. Her hands clamped to her head, as she paced the pool's edge.

Snu and Ebert sprang from the water, gasping for air. With his arm wrapped tight around Ebert's chest, Snu began to swim to the edge, dragging Ebert through the thick blackness. He struggled against the black film in the water, sliding under over and over. Stella ran to grab a long branch. Holding tightly to one end, she threw the other into the water near Snu. He grabbed hold and Stella pulled hard on the branch. Her feet slid out from under her as she pulled. She fell back. She scrambled to sit up and braced her feet in the dirt. Pulling again, she slid along the ground as she put all of her weight into the effort. The branch burned as it slid through her hands, but she didn't let go, only yanked harder and dug in her claws.

Snu finally reached the water's edge with Ebert. Stella dropped the branch and ran to help. She grabbed hold of Ebert and yanked him out of Snu's arms and onto the forest floor. She rolled him to his back. His eyes were closed.

"No," she screamed. "Ebert!"

As she shook Ebert to bring him to consciousness, the malped jumped onto Ebert. Its eyes glowed red and its hundreds of tiny legs sounded like they were beating on a drum as they banged on Ebert's chest. Stella grabbed the malped and tried to pull it off, but it hissed at her. It whipped its long tail around and hit her. Stella flew through the air and landed a few feet away. Snu, who had collapsed on the ground near the water, scrambled to his feet and ran towards Ebert. As he reached him, the malped jumped off and stood in front of Snu hissing and stopping Snu in his tracks. Stella ran from the other side and threw herself on top of Ebert to protect him. Everything went still, short, hysterical breaths escaped Stella.

Two hands shoved her hard. Stella looked down. Ebert was staring up at her. His nose twitched. His eyes were wide and frightened, with tears forming in their corners. Stella gasped and sat up. Ebert flung himself into her arms. Tears poured down Stella's face and as Ebert buried his own face in her chest, his shoulders heaved.

"He's fine. He will be fine… hisssss," the malped said as it slithered away from Snu towards Stella and Ebert.

"You saved him. You saved his life," Stella said between sobs.

The malped became very still and cocked its head sideways. It turned and walked away from them, laying a few feet away. Snu fell to his knees in front of Ebert and Stella. Stella pulled Snu to them and they sat, all three, piled on the forest floor and cried.

Eventually, Ebert broke free and wiped his eyes. His faced was covered in the black film, making the blue in his eyes shine brightly. Black goo dripped from his hair and slid down his cheeks like hot tar.

"I'm sorry," he whimpered, "I saw you leave this morning and followed you. I thought I could help," he hiccupped as he tried to breathe. "I thought the water was shallow and then it swallowed me," he sputtered as he began to cry again.

"You have been following us this whole time?" Snu asked.

Ebert nodded yes.

Stella stood and planted her hands on her hips. The adrenaline that had kept her going now slowly ebbed away. "You could have died, Ebert," she said quietly.

"I know," he sniffled. "But you saved me. I'm okay." Ebert forced a small smile.

Stella turned her back to him. She hung her head low and shook it slowly. She tried to still her breath, but she could not reply to Ebert. Her hands throbbed.

"I'm sorry," he tried again.

"It's okay, Ebert. You are safe now. That's all that matters," Snu said as he rubbed Ebert's back. Stella listened to Snu comfort her brother but did not turn back.

"Thank you for saving me, Snu," Ebert whispered.

"I just got you out of the water," Snu said. "I think it might have been the malped that saved you. When it jumped on you— whatever it did with its feet—it's like it brought your breath back."

Stella turned back to look at Snu and Ebert. Snu pointed to the malped lying a few feet away. It had gone to sleep.

"That? That creature saved me?" Ebert asked.

Stella nodded and sat back down with them. The fight had left her.

"What kind of a creature has power that can save like that?" she wondered.

Snu shook his head, "I don't know. But now we owe it Ebert's life."

CHAPTER 6

They had found a freshwater stream and were standing in it up to their ankles, cupping their hands and splashing water all over themselves quickly, trying to wash away the dirt and black slime that stuck to every inch of their bodies. They had found it too hard to move covered in the black goo, and so had stopped to free themselves from the sticky hold it had on them. Ebert sat a few arm-lengths away in the middle of the water, so exhausted that he was barely able to wash off the grime. The moon reflected on the water, lighting the space around them. Stella wondered when the moon had appeared. It floated in the sky above them, a slim crescent casting a radiant light onto the water. The heavy, gray clouds that had darkened the night sky had passed. Stella took comfort in the familiar sight; one she had enjoyed from the tree her whole life.

"What color is the stone?" Stella asked Snu.

"It's brown." He held the stone in the air above him. He carefully glanced at the malped, perched on the bank nearby.

"Brown? Warning color?" Stella asked.

"Yes. I guess we should just be glad it's not black anymore. I guess the alert of the black must have been because of Ebert."

"But it is still dark. Brown's not good."

"Of course it's not good. We are miles from the tree. Alone. In the middle of the carnage of the worst storm the Trebors have ever experienced. You didn't think it would be blue, did you?" Snu snapped.

Stella bristled at his words but grabbed his hands. "The malped didn't save Ebert—you did," she said. Snu sighed and dropped his shoulders.

"That was so close. We're lucky we got there in time," Snu replied.

"I know, but we did. Good thing you were with me," Stella smiled meekly. They had known each other their wholes lives. Their mothers were best friends, and so the two had been together since birth. For twelve years, they had been almost inseparable. Stella was now thankful he was with her. She didn't want to do this without him anymore.

"Thank you for coming with me," she said quietly. "I was wrong to try to keep you from coming. I couldn't have saved Ebert alone."

Snu smiled at Stella, making his square teeth glistened in a neat row. He gently extracted his hands out of Stella's to wash more as he spoke. "Me too, Stel. But I think we go back to the tree now. We almost lost Ebert trying to do this your way. We can't do it alone. We need the other Trebors to help us."

"We've come too far now to go back. Our fathers are out there, and they might need help. If we go back now, think of the time we are wasting!"

Snu shrugged. "Stella, this isn't safe, and you know it. And what about Ebert? He can't come with us."

"Please, Snu. Please, we have to keep going," Stella said.

"We can't take Ebert. You know what he's like. One minute he is impulsive and the next he's huddled and withdrawn," Snu whispered.

"He made it this far on his own, just following. He can do it. We can't go back, so he has to come. We can't send him home alone."

"I can hear you both," Ebert interjected. "I'll be fine. I can do it." He stood up with water dripping from his clothes and fur, and his blond hair streaked black. He hadn't made much progress getting clean.

Stella waded over to Ebert and grasped the wet fur on his shoulders. "This is not gonna be easy. You can't just do what you want. You have to stay with us. You have to listen, and you have to be strong."

"I can do those things," he replied. "And I can be useful. I want to find Yapa, too."

Stella looked at Snu and he raised in hands in surrender. She gently eased Ebert back down close to the water and began pouring water from her hands onto his head. Water streamed through her fingers and onto her brother's sleek, brown fur. Black muck ran from his fur and filled the water around them. Dirt eased from his hair and his long, bouncy curls freed themselves.

"Okay, you'll come with us," Stella said and then turned to look Snu. "That is, if we are still going?" She lifted her eyebrows.

Snu nodded his head yes, but his eyes darted away from Stella. Ebert put his arms around his sister so he could hug her tightly. Stella smiled.

"Any chance we can rest before we go, though?" Ebert asked.

Snu burst out laughing, and Stella felt a giddy feeling build in her chest. Ebert grinned as he looked from one to the other.

Stella smacked her hand on the water's surface, sending a spray of cool water all over Snu. He laughed harder and splashed back furiously. Soon all three were rolling in the water splashing and laughing. The black grime that had pooled around them from their clothes and fur drifted away and down the stream.

When they eventually pulled themselves together, they were spent and tired. Together they lay down by the stream's edge. Ebert curled up next to Stella, and it didn't take long for sleep to overtake him. Stella did not want to disturb him, so she lay there gazing at the moon. Snu snored loudly next to her. Unable to sleep, Stella thought of Yapa, wondering and worrying about what he was doing. They had an incredibly special bond, he understood her, made her feel special, and she wasn't sure what she would do if he didn't come home. The very thought of it made Stella short of breath and jumpy, and she looked around quickly to get her bearings.

Something cold and sharp brushed her cheek. Stella turned to see where the air came from. Inches from her face, the malped lurked. Stella jolted slightly.

"It will be full morning soon. The sun is cominnnng… hissss…" it said.

"I know, but Ebert needs sleep, and we all need a rest," she replied.

"You will not be able to go over the mountain when we get there. It will be light out by thenn… hisssss."

"I know. By the time we get to the bottom of the mountain now, it will be daytime for sure. We won't be able to climb the mountain without the other Trebors seeing us from the tree. We'll have to wait until night again before we can journey on."

"What if I were to tell you I have another way… hissss?"

"Another way over the mountain? One where the other Trebors won't see us?"

"Yessssssss…"

"But you told us you are lost. How could you know a new path?"

"Are we near your home?"

"My home. I am sure. Is gone."

"But you think you know another way?"

"It will be easier than going over the mountain, and you will not be seen if you go my wayyyyy… hissss"

Stella closed her eyes and thought. She did not want to be stuck waiting for nightfall to travel over the mountain. The idea of an easier path made her consider the pain in her knee and the soreness of her feet. She opened her eyes and looked back at the malped. Its eyes burrowed into hers.

"Let's take your path. When the others wake, we'll make our way to the base of the mountain and then follow your way." Even as she spoke Stella felt a chill of foreboding run through her. The lurking fatigue behind her eyes intensified and she could barely keep them open. Her decision somehow made her feel lonely. She pushed aside her uneasiness. The malped's legs pitter-pattered in reply as it backed away into the darkness.

Stella pushed herself as close to her brother as she could, but she still felt alone. The darkness around her seemed to creep into her bones. Her stomach ached and her knee throbbed. She wondered again if she was doing the right thing, and if the malped could really be trusted. She closed her eyes and as she drifted to sleep heard a voice saying, *"Go back to the tree…go back to the tree…"*

Suddenly, Yapa was in front of her. He wore a black crown and all of his fur was a shocking white. He stared at Stella and smiled, opening his arms for her embrace.

"Yapa! Yapa!" Stella screamed.

She leapt towards him, but just as her arms were about to engulf her father, he exploded. Cold air rushed up Stella's front and stood her hair on end. Red flashed in front of her eyes and a screeching noise tore at her ears. She stumbled back and fell to the ground. Her hands were numb and her face stung. She turned quickly to see where Yapa went but could see nothing. That's when she heard the words, *"Come, come."*

CHAPTER 7

Sun warmed Stella's skin, yet she shivered as she opened her eyes from her fitful sleep. Her rest had been full of nightmares and visions of her father, and now she was more tired than when she closed her eyes. Her lids were heavy, and her body ached. The arm Ebert had slept on was numb, and as she slipped it out from under him, pins and needles tingled all over her skin. The sky was bright and clear, but in the full light, the forest revealed an even starker scene than the night had. The harsh reality of the storm's destruction loomed heavy.

Snu was already awake and busy pulling a loaf of kasha bread and a pouch of flanuts out of his pack.

"Did you sleep okay?" she asked.

"I'm not sure. I feel terrible this morning. Everything aches."

"Me, too. You know it's the first night I've ever spent not sleeping in the tree," Stella said.

"Yeah, I guess that's true for me, too. When I sleep at home though I wake up refreshed. That definitely didn't happen this morning," Snu said. He shrugged as he handed Stella a handful of flanuts.

Stella took one flanut at a time and popped them into her mouth. Their bright orange color made her think of home, and the flat, round feeling in her mouth was a comfort. She relished the bright flavor and hoped the food would give her more energy. Ebert continued to snore nearby. Snu looked distant and tired. Stella wondered if she should tell Snu about seeing Yapa; but decided to just focus on getting to Mt. Bor and onto the malped's path.

"We should wake him up so we can get going soon," Stella said.

"Let him sleep a little more. Maybe he'll at least feel better when he wakes up," Snu said.

Stella pursed her lips and nodded. She wanted to get moving and was anxious to tell Snu about her conversation with the malped. She pushed her hand into the pouch of flanuts and pulled out a handful. She chewed them slowly, listening to her heartbeat in her ears.

"It's going to be fully daylight by the time we reach the bottom of the mountain. I don't think we're going to be able to climb to the other side today," Snu said.

Stella's pulse quickened as she hurried to reply, relieved Snu had brought up the mountain. "The malped has another path. He is going to lead us to the other side of the mountain. It's easier and the others won't see us," she blurted out.

Snu shook his head in disbelief and furrowed his brow, "An easier path? There's only one way—over."

"It's a long story. But the malped says it knows another way. You and I have never been over it in the first place or even to it, so it's not like we'd know if there was another path."

"But no other Trebor has ever talked about a way to the other side of the mountain other than over. We need to go *over* because that's our blind spot from the tree. Where our fathers could be."

"We'll get to the other side, we'll get to the blind spot, but just not over, on a different path."

Snu shook his head, "The malped knows another path—that's not over—to get to the other side?"

"Yes," Stella confirmed, trying to make her voice sound confident.

Snu rolled the guiding stone through his fingers in his pocket. His nose twitched. Stella wished she knew what he was thinking.

"It's bad enough that it's travelling with us. Now you want to follow it? Why do you find this new path so tempting? I don't know, what if I'm wrong and the tales are true. What if this "easier" path brings more danger or--,"

"You said they weren't real. You said there was no way the stories were true. Remember? That's why we are going to the other side of the mountain," Stella shouted.

"Stop yelling! I know I said that, but now that we are here, all alone, I'm not so sure anymore, something feels off," Snu replied.

"Even more reason to take the path of the malped then. If we don't, we wait for night and doesn't that sound worse?"

"I don't know Stel, easier doesn't always mean right or better. Day or night."

Stella felt desperate to have Snu agree with her, but she could see she wasn't going to win the argument at that moment. She thought of what she had seen the night before and shuddered. They couldn't waste time.

"Fine. Let's just get to Mt. Bor and then we can figure it out," she said slyly.

Snu squinted his eyes at Stella and got to his feet. He knew what she was thinking; they had known each other for too long. He took a few steps over to Ebert and rubbed the little Trebor's shoulder. "Time to wake up. We have to get moving," he whispered in Ebert's ear.

Ebert rolled over and his eyes snapped open. Recognition of where he was slowly spread across his face. His eyes scanned the devastated land around him. Stella wanted to grab him and pull him into a hug, but the anxious feeling that swirled in her head kept her rooted where she sat. She had never felt so useless before but pushed these feelings away and jumped to her feet. She handed Ebert the rest of her flanuts and faced Snu.

"Let's get moving," she said. The malped appeared next to her, its feet pitter- pattering. Stella rubbed her knee and stretched. The gnawing pain in her knee, soreness in her hands, and stabbing in her stomach did not ease, but they needed to move.

They travelled more slowly than they had the night before. The naïve assumption that the journey would lead to quick success had left Stella and she felt drained. Stella had not lost hope completely, but the further they travelled from the tree, the more alone she felt. They walked for hours with the malped leading them. Stella's feet burned and her eyes were so sore it was hard to see through the stream of constant tears. Her knee throbbed. Her exhaustion made her increasingly impatient with Ebert's moaning and Snu's silence. She had tried several times to help Snu see why following the new path was a good idea, but he had only kept his stride steady and his eyes on the terrain ahead. She tried to stay composed, but even Snu's stoic demeanor was starting to wear thin. Stella was about to lash out at the Ebert and Snu when they reached a body of water so vast it spanned miles on either side. They could see the other side of the water, but to the right and left, it stretched on and on.

"It's gonna to take hours to make our way around," Snu said.

"I can't even see where it ends," Ebert added.

A fierce gust of wind blew, and Ebert struggled to stay on his feet.

"What's it doing?" Snu asked. The group looked towards the water, where the malped was floating on a piece of bark. The wind drove the bark towards the middle of the water.

"Like thisssss," the malped hissed.

Stella looked at Snu. They both looked at Ebert.

"What?" Ebert asked.

"Look at the malped. We could go across the water if we find more bark to float on," Stella said.

"But... I... the black..." Ebert stammered.

"It's okay, we'll be together. We can make our way around the black patches, and when we can't, we can push the float through," Snu replied.

"I'm scared," Ebert said in a small voice.

"The wind will help. Look, it's already blown the malped to the other side," Stella said. Another gust of wind blew her hair over her face and her fur bristled so she pushed her fur back roughly. As the wind blew, the water rippled towards the bank on the other side where the malped had curled into a ball, asleep. Stella felt comforted by its easy rest and grateful that it had shown them how to get across.

Together, Stella, Snu and Ebert found a charred piece of tree bark and pulled it to the edge of the water. They grabbed twigs to push through the black film. With great force, they heaved the bark into the water. Stella jumped onboard; Ebert stepped in timidly, and Snu shoved their watercraft as he bounded onto the back. The bark tipped back and forth violently as Snu got settled. He was not a small Trebor.

The skin under Ebert's fur was no longer pink, but a shocking white.

"Breathe Ebert. Breathe. We'll be there in no time," Stella reassured him. He sat, glassy eyed, focusing hard on the malped on the far side.

Stella smiled as a wild wind picked up the back of the bark and propelled it forward. The force was so strong that the bark cut through the sludgy, black film, sending them straight to the middle of the water. Snu cheered. Another gust of wind blew in behind them, but the force of it was unwieldy. The bark rocked viciously, spraying black film all over them. Stella leant over Ebert and mopped black muck from his forehead. He still did not move. His claws dug into the bark. The rocking stopped. Snu and Stella used their twigs to push through the heavy black sludge. Their progress was painfully slow, and the ache in Stella's hands grew unbearable. Scabs ripped open again, and the raw skin felt like it was burning. Snu stopped to rest. There was no wind. The bark drifted slowly parallel to the shore but did not shift towards the bank.

"We can't stop. We are drifting the wrong way," Stella cried.

Snu thrust his twig deep into the water. A fresh, powerful gust of wind snapped up the edge of the water and sent a massive wave rolling towards them. Panic surged through Stella's arms. She pushed at the water manically. The wave hit them with such force that the back of the bark lifted out of the water. The bark flipped over. Ebert collided into Stella as they flew through the air. He bounced off her into the water. Stella sank next to him. All three quickly bobbed to the surface. Stella grabbed hold of Ebert's fur and dragged him to her.

Snu swam towards the bark, threw his body on top of it, and began pushing it towards them. Ebert climbed on and lay on his stomach. Snu and Stella lay with their bodies half in the water and half on the bark and kicked. They went nowhere. They could not get their legs to push through the black mire that encased them. Then the wind blew again, more gently this time, and they inched to the shore. Stella rested her forehead against the bark.

"Please blow again. Please send us the right way," she yelled. Another great gust came. They flew out of the water, clinging to the bark, claws digging deep into the wood. Again, they flipped in the air but this time flew forward, twirling in the hurricane of wind. The wind stopped and all at once dropped the bark and its occupants. They bounced to a stop inches from the malped, which raised its head and blinked at them. Its legs ran their rhythm and it smiled.

"Good, you made itttttt," the malped said calmly.

"You made it! You made it? That's what you say to us?" Snu hollered. The skin under his fur burned red. He clutched his pocket as he yelled, his hand wrapped protectively around the guiding stone. It was still there, safe.

"It was the best wayyyyy," the malped said.

Snu glared at the malped. Stella pushed herself to her feet and patted Snu's back.

"Leave it alone," she said, exhaustion pulling at her voice. "The malped didn't make us do that. It wasn't its fault."

"We made it," Ebert's small voice echoed. Stella wondered if she heard relief or fear in Ebert's voice. He smiled at her briefly, and she decided to assume it was relief.

The malped pushed itself up with its front arms and surveyed the land ahead of them. Stella shook her whole body and black-tinged water flew from her fur. She pointed to the mountain.

"We're close. We don't have too much further until we reach the mountain," she said.

Wet, angry, and drained they regrouped and pushed forward towards the mountain. In and out of the thicket of dense debris, they forced a path. The sun rose high above them and beat down mercilessly. Every few steps, they had to stop to drink water from their packs and rest. Stella's head swirled and pounded. She longed to be back at the tree. As she tripped over another exposed root, she thought of her home, her bed, and Yama. She wondered how much the tree had grown new leaves and whether the elders had noticed. She should have tried harder to get them to notice. With a new burst of energy, she decided she would tell Snu it had all been a terrible mistake. They should turn back. And then the forest ended.

As they stepped out of the forest, a giant field stretched before them. The mountain loomed behind it, a stony, smoky goliath reaching into the sky. From the tree, Stella had always enjoyed watching the giant birds circle its peaks, but as she looked now, there were no birds. The sky was clear and blue, but nothing soared overhead except trails of smoke from smoldering patches of earth that spread all over the mountain.

"It's so strange," Snu said. "How is there a cleared field in the middle of the forest?"

"It's so smooth, and flat, and black," Ebert said.

Stella couldn't pull her eyes away from the strange sight. The storm had left its stain: the field was singed and dark like the rest of the forest floor. But there were no jagged branches or brambles, no upturned trees.

"What's that?" Ebert asked, his nose twitching as he pointed in the distance towards Mt. Bor.

Stella squinted to see what Ebert was pointing at. Snu strained to get a glimpse as well. A big and round, tree trunk stood at the far end of the clearing. It rose towards the sky, until suddenly it didn't. The giant trunk stopped as though someone had cut it in half. There were no branches growing from the trunk; and as far as Stella could see there was no debris on the ground around it. How had the trunk not been blown over or destroyed in the storm like all of the other trees? It was a lone column, an eerie survivor. It was the only thing left standing other than their home, their own mighty tree. And yet, unlike their tree, this one had no green hue or brightness springing from its bark.

Stella's knee began to pound again, and she leaned down and rub it. Even the motion of leaning over exhausted her. Her stomach ached and her sore hands now felt stiff. She put them to her cheek. They felt like ice. She clenched her fists and released them, shaking her hands as she turned to speak to Snu.

"It's strange isn't it? I wonder how it survived the storm," she pondered. Snu did not respond. Instead a shadow settled over his face. Stella felt suddenly like he was miles away from her. He, too, shook his hands.

"Let's go and see!" Ebert squealed and threw himself at full speed into the open field.

"No. Stop!" Stella yelled, but it was too late. He was already barreling forward with puffs of soot trailing behind him. Stella and Snu chased after him. They choked on the smoky trail he left in his wake. They gained on Ebert quickly, and Stella seized his arm to bring him to a stop.

"You can't do that! You can't run away! Don't you remember what happened? Don't you remember how close you were to dying!" She shrieked. "Don't you understand that you have to be careful? Can't you just wait for once and listen to us?"

Snu put his hand on Stella's shoulder. "I think he gets it Stella."

She shoved his hand from her shoulder; she didn't want reassurance.

"No, no, he doesn't get it. Look at him. His nose is twitching. His eyes are gleaming. He's glad he ran. I've had enough. Enough!"

"I'm sorry, Stella. I just wanted to see that strange tree trunk," Ebert mumbled. Stella grunted and released Ebert's arm. He gave her a wounded stare as he rubbed the place she had grasped.

"Don't you see that I can make my own path too, Stella? Why do you get to push away the other Trebors and not listen to the code, but when I don't follow your plan you get upset with me!" Ebert yelled.

Stella took a step back. Her brother had a wild look in his eyes, and his voice was sharp and biting. His words stung as the truth of them hit her hard.

"He has a point, Stel. It's not that different from you wanting Yama to let you make your own path, from you wanting Yama and the elders to listen to you," Snu said.

"I'm useful too! See me!" Ebert hollered louder.

Stella's face burned.

"Stooooooop……" hissed the malped. Stella had forgotten about the malped and was now surprised to see it standing next to her speaking.

"No more fighting… we must move forward… to the mountainnnnnn"

Stella forced herself to turn her attention from Ebert. She narrowed her eyes to take in the malped.

"No more. We need to go home," she replied.

"No…. can'tttttt turn back now… I can show you the path… it will be easy… it will be quick… other side… we will get there… hissssss."

"The only path I see is that narrow line that runs up the mountain. I can't see any other way!" Stella's shrill voice had become hysterical, and she tried to calm herself. A flare of fear and loneliness lit in her chest at having to make another decision. She pointed to the thin line weaving up the side of the mountain, snaking from side-to-side and disappearing over the top.

"There is another way. Will you follow meeeee… hissss?" the malped asked.

Stella saw Ebert gazing at the mountain, his jaw slack. He had withdrawn now. Stella had yelled too much. Snu was staring at the mountain as well, his hands on his hips, his face unreadable. Stella struggled to keep the panic in her chest from taking over.

"Where, malped, is this other path?" Stella asked.

"Followwwwww… hisssssss."

The malped's body rolled forward as its tiny legs quickly moved it along the field's earth. Snu grabbed Ebert's hand and followed. Stella stood and watched. She shook her hands to try to warm them.

Snu looked over his shoulder. "Are you coming?" he asked.

Stella took a step forward and looked at the mountain peak. Still no birds. The ache in her stomach grew so she reached into her backpack to grab a piece of kasha bread. Shoving it in her mouth, she began to walk. She chewed as she walked but a lump rose in her throat that made it hard to swallow the bread. She fought to calm herself and she struggled to swallow. She deliberately trailed behind the others, giving herself time to regroup, hoping she'd feel better with the food. Snu's steps were slower as well, and Ebert had lost the spunk that had propelled him into the field. Only the malped's legs moved quickly, seeming to move faster the closer they got to the mountain. Every few minutes, it would turn to look at Stella. Its eyes would meet hers as it cocked its head. Stella would nod back, and the malped would continue moving. She could not shake the solitude and aching that settled into her bones.

They eventually reached the strange, broken tree trunk. The bark was black, and when Stella put her hand on it, it was cold and rough. It somehow smelled dark. The trunk cast a deep shadow that sprawled across the field behind it. The malped climbed up the side of the trunk and clung to it a few feet above Stella's head.

"This was once a grand tree. It stretched to great heightssssss… hiss."

"What happened to it?" Stella asked.

"It grew too large. There wassss a single bolt of lightning… thisssss is all that remainsssss… it has stood like this for as long as I can rememberrrrr…..hissssss," the malped answered.

Stella noticed Ebert sitting at her feet, staring up at the malped. His nose twitched, and his fingers clawed at the earth next to him. His eyes darted in all directions. She worried about what might be running through his mind and whether he felt relieved or emboldened by the truthful words he had hurled at her.

She turned back to the malped. "And yet this storm left it standing, while it destroyed almost everything else in its path. It doesn't seem right. And how do you know this? Is this your home?"

The malped ignored her as it climbed back down slowly. It stopped at eye level with Stella. "I will show you now… the paaaaaath."

Stella gave her hands another quick shake and wiggled her fingers. Snu had wandered away around the trunk. She yelled for him to come back. As he made his way towards her, his steps were flat and his head hung low, his ears dropped. Stella turned back to the malped. It was gone.

"Ebert, did you see where the malped went?" she asked.

Ebert did not speak, but instead pointed to the top of the trunk. Stella took a step back and tilted her head up. She did not see the malped.

"What were you yelling about? I was checking out this trunk. Its diameter is almost as big as our tree's. It's huge. But yet, it stops so abruptly, it doesn't look natural," Snu said as he approached Stella and Ebert.

Stella nodded distractedly as she kept her gaze on the top of the trunk. Where was the malped? It seemed to have vanished into thin air.

"What are you doing?" Snu asked.

Stella's shoulders sagged as she turned to Snu. "It's gone. The malped. One minute it said it would show us the path and the next it's gone."

Snu snickered and sank down next to Ebert. He gave Ebert a quick pat on the back before reaching into his pack for food. "Perfect," he snorted. He pulled out two rumple fruits. "Just perfect," he repeated as he peeled the first rumple in one long, red spiral.

CHAPTER 8

Red juice from the rumple fruit dribbled down Ebert's chin. He smiled as he wiped it away with the back of his fist, his fur instantly red and sticky. Stella fought the urge to tell him to stop making a mess, but he obviously didn't want her to tell him what to do anymore. Had she really been treating him the way she felt the tribe treated her and dismissed him like they did her? The thought made her feel both confused and angry.

"*It's not the same*," she said to herself. But the nagging sting of his words and the malped's disappearance made Stella feel unbalanced. She felt very distant from Snu, Ebert, and everything from home. She had been so sure of her mission when she left the tree; but now, she was filled with doubt and her confidence waned. Still, an angry bubble rose in her chest as she watched Snu and Ebert eat. It was them. They were the reason the journey wasn't working. She should have done this alone.

As she stewed, she watched Snu hand piece after piece of rumple to Ebert. He ignored her glares. She wondered if she should tell them to go home and leave her to finish this trip alone. Snu struggled with his pack, unable to close it. He wrestled to pull the links together, but they wouldn't catch. He pulled and tugged.

"What is wrong with your pack?" Stella blurted out. He lifted his head and briefly locked eyes with her before dropping his gaze back to the pack. Stella rolled her eyes and snatched the pack from him, seeing that he hadn't noticed that something was stuck in the links.

"Here, let me," she barked.

Stella grabbed the pull and yanked. The zipper didn't budge. She examined it closely and saw the tip of something small and brown stuck in the grooves of the links. She tugged back the pull, held the small piece, and yanked at it. Out of Snu's pack came a tiny branch with little buds lining its smooth bark. Stella held the branch in her hand and rubbed the tiny green leaves. She felt warmth run through her fingers. She looked at Snu and asked, "Is this from home?"

Snu's face went bright red. He turned his eyes to the ground and nodded, his spikey hair bounced.

"You brought a branch from the tree in your pack?" she demanded.

"I thought it would remind me of home. I know it seems strange, but when I'm scared, I rub my fingers along its bark and I feel better," Snu replied.

Stella rubbed her fingers along the branch and felt the ache in her stomach start to subside and her fingers warm. The branch had a deep, earthy smell that tickled her nose. Relief flooded over her as she drew in the rich smell of home, but suddenly her unbalanced emotions snatched away her joy and left a dark, resentful feeling in its place.

"It's like you brought a blankie from home," Stella jeered. She didn't know why she felt so bitter, or why she would say such a hurtful thing to her best friend, but she couldn't stop herself.

"You know what, Stel, that's really mean. I didn't want to feel too far from home. I didn't want to feel alone, so I took a branch from the top of the tree. What is wrong with you? Why are you being so awful?"

"It feels like you should be stronger than that," Stella said. "Like you don't need to have something like that to make you feel better."

"Are you telling me you didn't feel anything when you touched it?"

"Stop badgering me! We don't have time for this. We need a plan; we don't need rumble fruit and tree branches!"

Stella glowered at Snu, whose eyes were shining with anger. The fur on the back of his neck stood up; she had never seen him so upset with her before. "Stella, this isn't just about you, and there is nothing wrong with having something from home. It keeps me feeling connected."

"I'm *sorry*. I didn't realize you would take this all the wrong way."

"The wrong way? You called it my blankie. What was the right way I was supposed to take it? I love our home. The tree protected us and saved us from destruction. It proved to me that it's worth holding on to a piece of that safety! You know what? I keep putting you before the tribe, and it's time I stop. If we had stayed at our tree and worked with the other Trebors, we'd have help right now and a real plan. Instead, we're lost and alone!"

Stella fell silent. She couldn't think of how to reply. She felt embarrassed that she had made fun of Snu and wondered why she had been so quick to disregard his feelings. Snu grabbed the branch out of her hand and shoved it back in his pack. The pulls worked easily along the links now as he hurried to cinch it closed. When he was done, he stormed away from Stella.

"Snu... I..." Stella tried to speak but her words fell into the wide pit in her stomach.

"It's time I change. Maybe you should too, Stella," Snu called, his voice flat. Ebert scampered after him.

As Snu marched off, Stella stood very still. The cold crept back into her hands and a piercing pain crept up her leg. When she looked down, she saw that her knee was freshly bleeding. She didn't remember banging it again, but the pain that returned felt as though she had just fallen on it. She squeezed her eyes shut and made fists with her hands, opening and closing them. It did little to stop the pain. She squatted, exhausted, and flopped backwards to lay flat on the ground looking at the sky. Snu was right. So was Ebert. Why hadn't she understood before? A bolt of regret shot through her. She felt defeated and empty.

"I shouldn't have left the tree and tried to do this my way," Stella whispered. "I give up. I should have trusted the tree and my tribe!" The sky above was as blank as she felt.

Then she noticed a small black dot in the sky. At first, it seemed to stay in place, but the longer she watched it, the bigger it became. Slowly she made out the shape of a bird. It was enormous with a wingspan greater than anything she had ever seen. Flashes of red and yellow streaked the sky; its plumage was vibrant and caught the sun as it circled in the air above her.

Stella searched the sky for other birds, but it was alone. As the bird flew closer, she saw it had a bright crest of feathers on its head. Its eyes seemed fixed on her. She lay still, mesmerized. The bird circled closer. Stella could see the scales on its legs. It got closer still and she noticed the gold tips of its wings. And still it flew towards her. Still she did not move. The bird had something in its mouth, but Stella couldn't see what it was. Soon the giant bird was within a few feet of Stella's frozen body. Its eyes were a bright piercing blue that sparkled amid its dark feathers. The bird locked eyes with Stella as it swooped past her. Its feathers grazed the tips of her toes. She could feel the air rustle around her as it passed. The bird soared back up into the sky and slowly, slowly became a small black dot again. Then it was gone. All that lingered was a faint song that blew away with the wind.

Stella sat up and looked on her lap. She was covered in tiny green leaves. They glowed with the same iridescence she had seen from the top of her tree. She scooped up a handful and held them to her face. They smelled like home, fresh and alive. Her hands were no longer cold. She chose a leaf and rubbed it on her knee. The skin tingled and felt warm then the throbbing stopped. Stella's heart began to race. She picked up every leaf the bird had dropped and shoved them into her pack. She rushed over to Snu and Ebert, sitting nearby.

She beamed at them. "Wasn't that amazing?"

"What?" Snu asked.

"The bird. I've never seen anything like it! It was magnificent," Stella exclaimed.

Snu and Ebert peered up at the sky.

"I don't see any birds," Ebert said.

"You didn't see the bird that just flew past us? It almost landed on me!"

"Are you feeling okay?" Snu asked, the edge in his voice gone, a concerned look on his face there now instead. "You were lying in the sun for some time, maybe you might need some water and shade. Here, sit down." He patted the ground next to him.

Stella slid down between Snu and Ebert and leaned back onto the trunk. Her head felt like it was spinning. She opened her mouth to tell them about the leaves, but slowly shut it again.

"You didn't see any birds?" she finally asked.

"Here. Drink this," Snu said, handing her his water and shaking his head no.

Stella took a long drink of water and examined her knee. There was no blood. Not only had the pain stopped, but a new scab had formed over the giant gash and the swelling was gone. She rubbed it. When it didn't hurt, her heart fluttered and she grinned. She felt happy and reenergized. She didn't understand why the others hadn't seen the bird, but she didn't think it mattered. She had, and it gave her new hope. Stella rose to her feet and finished the rest of the water in one long gulp. She studied Mt. Bor as she drank.

"Are you feeling better?" Ebert asked.

"Oh yes, fine. Just fine. Snu's right, I must have had too much sun. And I'm sorry. I was terrible before," Stella stammered. "You're both right. I've seen only me."

"That's okay," Snu said graciously. "I'm just glad that you're okay now. You kind of scared me before. All that talk of a bird flying at you…" Snu bumped his shoulder against Stella's. Ebert hugged her.

"Yeah, sun, dehydration, you were right," Stella said. She avoided making eye contact with Snu.

In a hurry to change the subject, Stella pointed to the mountain, "I don't understand where the malped went and I certainly don't see any other path other than the narrow one that leads over the mountain. And by now our mothers must have alerted the whole tribe that we are gone. They will have lookouts—they are bound to see us if we are on the face of the mountain while it is light out."

"I knew we shouldn't trust that malped," Snu said, shaking his head. "He promised us an easier path, one that would keep us out of view and get us more quickly to the other side of the mountain… It was too good to be true."

"I wish it were true. I want to see Yapa," Ebert whimpered.

Stella wrapped her arms around her brother and hugged him tightly. As Ebert reached his arms around his sister, his foot got caught on a root and he lurched forward. Arm-in-arm the two tumbled into the rough bark of the old trunk. It scratched Stella's back, but it didn't stop their fall. They kept falling. They fell further backwards and then head over heels, again and again. They flew through the air, gaining speed, around and around. Stella felt her stomach rise into her throat and her legs tingled. Ebert screamed and she held him tightly. Though her head was spinning, she was scared to let go of him. Suddenly she felt her body bounce and come to a stop. When she put her hand down, she felt a lush, bed of moss under her. A bright light surrounded them as a glowing cloud rose from the bed of moss. The cloud hovered over their heads. Stella reached up to touch the cloud and it spun into motion: it wasn't a cloud at all, but hundreds of glowing, chalky moths. They took flight, whipping round and round to form a tornado of flapping wings. Up they climbed, the soft beating of wings echoing in the hollow space inside the trunk, higher and higher they flew until they became one with the dark and disappeared from sight. Only the whooshing noise remained, hanging in the air above Stella and Ebert. They could see nothing. It was pitch black.

"Where are we?" Ebert's asked, his voice trembling.

Stella glanced around to get her bearings, but all she could see was a small light high above them. "We must have fallen through a hole in the trunk. Can you see it? The small light up there? That must have been where we fell from. We're inside." She made her voice sound even and unconcerned, but even she could hear the shakiness in her words.

"Stella? Stella… Ebert? Ebert…?" a voice echoed around them, the words faint.

"Did you hear that? I think it's Snu," Stella said. Ebert began to cry quietly. Stella pulled him close.

"Snu? Snu!" she yelled, but her voice disappeared above her.

There was no reply.

Ebert sobbed, his little body shook terribly and his nose twitching so quickly that it frightened Stella.

"It's okay, it's okay. We just have to climb back up to the hole. Feel those claws of yours—you can climb anything. Let's climb back up and find Snu. It's going to be okay."

Stella pulled Ebert to his feet and they stumbled, blinded by the darkness, until they hit the wall of the trunk. Stella reached out and rubbed her hand along the inside of the trunk bark. To her surprise, it was rough and cold, not smooth and warm like the inside of her tree. She reached up and stretched out her claws to begin the climb. Ebert did the same.

"*Ahhhhhh!*" Stella screamed and dropped off the wall. Two red eyes glowed in front of her. Ebert jumped from the wall and wrapped his arms around Stella, shaking. Stella turned her head slowly. To her horror, there were hundreds, maybe thousands, of tiny red eyes, each glowing and shiny, and each directing its attention on them. The eyes spread around the inside of the trunk. Stella couldn't see any bodies, just eyes.

"They are everywhere and they're getting closer!" Ebert screamed as he tightened his grip around Stella's waist.

Stella's heart was pounding so hard she had trouble catching her breath. Beads of sweat sprouted on her forehead. The eyes were getting closer. Tiny red dots floated in front of them. Stella swung her arms around wildly trying to touch something, trying to scare the eyes away, but she felt nothing. She swung harder. Ebert dropped his arms from her waist and began to do the same.

"Leave us alone!" she shouted. "Leave us alone!"

A cold chill ran down her spine as she turned to see a set of eyes within inches of her face. She punched the air in front of her, but the eyes dodged her punches. She tried again. The eyes moved. With each swing, Stella touched nothing—the eyes just moved a few inches from her hands. She felt like they were taunting her, tempting her to keep trying, like she was part of a game.

"What are you? What do you want?" she screamed.

Pitter patter, pitter patter, silence. Pitter patter, pitter patter, silence. Pitter patter, pitter patter, pitter patter…

"Hello?" she said quietly.

"What is that noise? I've heard it before," Ebert whispered.

"Stellaaaaaa… hissssssss…"

"Is that the malped?" Ebert asked.

The red eyes all stayed still. They no longer seemed to be moving towards them.

"Is that you malped?" Stella called, her voice quivering.

"Yesssssssss… don't be afraid… you are with friends… these are my fellow malpeds… they were just curious… they have never seen a Trebor before… I'm sorry if they scaaaared you… hisssss."

"Why are you here? Where are we?" Stella yelled. She scanned the space around her, trying to see the malped.

"I left you outside the trunnnnnk to check the path I spoke of… and I found my fellow malpeds here."

"Where are you?" Stella shouted.

She flinched as something landed on her arm. Tiny little taps ran in a rhythm up and down her arm. A shiver took over her body, and she shook her arm violently to stop the feeling. Slowly, the malped's shape formed around his red eyes. His skin became the same color of her fur, no longer taking on the blackness of the space around them. Stella felt its feet moving rhythmically along her arm and she shivered again. She turned to Ebert. He looked small and scared. She peered back at the malped, and it cocked its head to the side to return her gaze.

"What's happening? Where are we? Is this your home?"

"Nooooooo… the other malpeds just took cover here… after I was swept away from them… hissssss."

Stella stared at the malped, waiting for more, but it said nothing else. Finally, Stella decided the malped was the only help she had. She broke the silence.

"We lost Snu. We fell through a hole and he is still outside," she said.

"Ah… yesssssss… you stumbled into a door… how unfortunate Snu didn't come with you… hisssss," the malped replied.

"Can you help us get back to him and then show us the path?"

"Yes… I will hellllp…" The malped leapt from Stella's arm and she watched as its skin slowly disappear into the dark.

"Hisssss… hissss…" The malped called. The noise was different from the voice it had used to talk to her. As it made this noise, all of the red eyes began to merge. What had been hundreds of tiny eyes now looked like two, huge, red eyes. They loomed over Stella and Ebert. Ebert gripped Stella's hand tightly.

"FOLLOW!" A loud voice boomed.

The red eyes began to rise. Stella and Ebert climbed along the inside of the trunk. They moved quickly together, each moment getting closer to the light of the hole they had come through. Stella focused on each move she made, making sure she stayed close to Ebert as they climbed. When they reached an area below the opening, the red eyes stopped and hovered above them.

A sharp sound pierced the air, followed by the same loud voice, "GO!" It screeched.

CHAPTER 9

Stella shoved Ebert through the opening and scurried out after him. They collapsed on the blackened ground. The malped leapt onto the earth beside them. The bright sunlight outside was jarring, and Stella squinted to see Ebert. She struggled to catch her breath as her heart raced. Ebert lay on the ground next to her, his chest rising and falling quickly, his breathing labored, his eyes sealed shut. Stella reached out and slid her hand on top of his clenched fists. Eventually the normal rhythm of her breathing returned, and she felt Ebert pull his hand from hers. She opened her eyes to check on him and felt the uneasy breathing take hold again as she watched him sitting silently staring ahead, with glassy eyes and a twitching nose.

Stella struggled to find the right thing to say, something that would calm him. But all she could hear was the voice in her head wishing they weren't alone, wishing she could get them both out of this awful situation and back to the safety of the tree. She gulped hard to tamp down her own fears, hoping Ebert wouldn't notice her exhaustion and insecurity.

"Where's Snu?" Ebert said.

Snu! Stella thought and jumped to her feet. She swung around quickly, looking in all directions. "Snu? Snu!" she yelled. *How had she not noticed sooner?*

Ebert was on his feet now, too, yelling manically, "Snu! Where are you? Where are you…?"

"He must be looking for us. He probably just ran around the trunk to the other side. I'm sure he's just searching," Stella said as her head swirled.

Ebert began to run around the trunk. Stella followed, and the malped glided alongside.

"Snu…" they yelled repeatedly.

"Where is he?" Ebert's voice begged.

"Keep going. He can't have gone far. I'm sure he was worried about us," Stella replied.

They looped around the entire trunk and then stopped where they started. Stella put her hands on her knees, leaned over, and inhaled deeply to catch her breath. "We should just wait here. It's no use going around again," she huffed.

"Snu," Ebert yelled again. "Where are you?"

Stella took another breath. Ebert kept yelling.

"Commmmme… we'll look from on hiiiiigh…" the malped hissed loudly. It climbed up the side of the trunk.

"Yes. Good. Come on Ebert," Stella wheezed.

She dug her claws into the trunk's bark and climbed deliberately. Impatient, Ebert quickly climbed past her. He stopped further up the trunk and yelled frantically.

"I still can't see him!" Ebert banged his head against the trunk's rough bark and groaned. Stella scrambled over to him. She leaned her face close to his. Tears filled his eyes and his breathing was shallow and weak. Stella fought to hold back her own tears. She tried to form words to comfort him, but again found she was empty. She ran the back of her hand across her forehead to push her hair from her eyes. Her skin prickled and her eyes were suddenly heavy. Ebert continued to moan.

"I do not seeeeeee himmmmmm…." the malped called out. It was perched high above them, its view much better than theirs.

"He left us," Ebert whispered. He did not pick up his head or look at Stella.

"No, Ebert. He wouldn't leave us," Stella replied quickly.

"Then where is he? He's disappeared. Now we're even more alone."

"I'm sure he is looking for us, Ebert. Or maybe he went back for help. Come on, let's climb down. Let's take a break and wait."

Stella pulled at Ebert's shoulder and tried to loosen his claws from the bark, but he suddenly turned and screamed at her, "He's dead, Stella! Dead! Like Yapa! Gone!"

A flush of heat burned Stella's hands and face and she staggered away from Ebert. His eyes bore into her. They were dull and no light shone from them. Stella scrambled away down the trunk, or maybe she fell, she couldn't tell, she was numb. The darkness she saw in Ebert shook her to her core, but that was nothing compared to the fear she felt that Snu might actually be gone for good. Like Yapa? Was Yapa gone? Had she lost them both? Home. She had to get them back to the tree. She dropped to her knees and put her face in her hands. How could this have gone so wrong? How could she be so alone and confused?

A heavy weight pushed against Stella's head, arms surrounded her and squeezed. "I'm sorry Stella," Ebert's voice whispered. "I don't know what happened to me."

Stella let herself cry. Her shoulders shook, and she collapsed into her brother. His tiny arms held her tightly and the feeling of them pushing into her made her cry even harder. She let herself squeal and moan, and still Ebert held her with a strength she did not know he had. She let him hold her together until she was wrung empty, and only then did she pick up her head to look at Ebert. The light in his eyes was back and he smiled a shy smile at her.

"I'm sorry," he said again.

"Me too," Stella replied. She had doubted her brother, but now she could see how she needed him, too. The realization made her feel suddenly lighter and less alone. It also made it clear to her what they needed to do.

"We have to go back to the tree," she said, her voice tired. "We can't do this alone. The only way to find Snu and Yapa is to go and ask for help. I was wrong to think I could do all of this alone."

"Not alonnnnnne…" the malped mused. "I am here… I will hellllp."

Stella had forgotten that the malped was nearby. She turned to look at it, "I know you mean well, but what can you do? You need to go back to the other malpeds and find your way home with them. There were so many of them in the trunk before, together you will be able to get back. Go to them. I need to take Ebert back to the tree and tell the elders what has happened."

The malped's eyes seemed to change colors as Stella spoke. The bright red color she had grown accustomed to was replaced by a gold color with flecks of red. Stella found herself unable to look away.

"*Go*, malped. This is not your problem!" she yelled, but even as she spoke, she could not take her eyes from the malped. A dizzy feeling swirled in her head.

The malped walked backwards with his eyes locked on Stella's. Stella followed. Ebert crept carefully behind them. Stella followed the malped around the trunk, unable to take her gaze from its eyes. The malped's eyes seemed to will her forward step by step. When the eyes returned to their normal red, Stella shook her head and the dizzy feeling slipped away.

"Why did you bring us here? Didn't you hear anything I said?" she asked.

"Loooooook," the malped turned its head towards a strange marking on the trunk. Stella studied the design, looking closely at the lines that were deeply grooved into the bark. She ran her fingers along them, tracing the pattern.

"It's a leaf!" Ebert exclaimed from behind Stella. Stella took a step back and looked. It was a leaf.

"I show you the paaaaath nowwwww…. to the other side of the mountainnnn…"

"This leaf is the path?" Stella asked.

"It's the doorrr," the malped replied.

"I told you. We're going back to the tree. I need help to find Snu. I can't do this alone." Stella turned to leave again. She stopped when she heard the malped's voice, which was deeper, more insistent.

"Snu might have used this door into the trunk. We cannot see him for miles. It is the only explanationnnn…"

Stella froze. It hadn't occurred to her that Snu might have tried to find them by seeking another way into the trunk they had fallen into. Perhaps he had gone this way. As she contemplated her options, she noticed a shimmer on the ground next to her. She knelt down to inspect it and quickly threw her hand to her chest when she saw what it was. She scraped the soot to the side. It was the guiding stone. It was so very black that she would have missed it if it weren't for the sun catching it for a moment. Stella brushed the stone off on her leg and looked at it more closely. There was no doubt it was the guiding stone. Snu must have been there. She wrapped her hand around the stone.

She turned to the malped, "Are you sure you can help us? Are you sure you don't want to go back to the other malpeds?"

"Yesssssssss," it hissed.

Stella placed her hand over the leaf markings on the bark. She pushed. A door swung open and a cool breeze swept over them, even though a damp smell hung in the air.

"Are we going? Do you think Snu is in there?" Ebert asked.

"I don't know," Stella replied. "But it's our only option. He must've been here."

Ebert took the stone from Stella's hand and looked at it closely. "Can I keep it with me?" Stella nodded yes, held his hand, and together they stepped through the door.

Inside the door, Ebert and Stella stood on a large platform that jutted out into the center of the trunk. As their eyes adjusted slowly to the dim lighting, Stella noticed tiny holes in the trunk walls. Thin streaks of sunlight filtered through to barely illuminate the giant space. More platforms like the one they stood on stuck out from walls, going up as high as she could see. Giant webs hung between the platforms.

Tiny beads of water slowly dripped from them and disappeared into the darkness below them. Spilling out on the platforms were tables and chairs, toys and books. Large rooms were burrowed into the thick walls next to the platforms, creating living spaces that looked eerily similar to her own home. Except, unlike her home, this space was completely silent. All she could hear was Ebert breathing loudly next to her and the malped's feet tapping on the boards below their feet. The space smelled damp and moldy. Stella shuddered against the coldness that tickled her arms.

"Hello?" Ebert yelled into the cavernous space. His voice echoed back… "hello… hello… hello…." He looked at Stella, puzzled.

"I thought someone might live here," he said as if to explain himself. "But no one replied."

"It looks like it was abandoned. Maybe those tales of another tribe were true. Maybe they were here. But where'd they go? It looks like they left in a hurry," Stella said.

"Do you think the stories of great danger are true then? A giant evil creature?" Ebert asked.

"No time… no time…" the malped exclaimed. "We must keep movingggg."

"But what happened here? Who lived here?" Stella asked.

"I don't knowwwwwww… I only knowwwww the path…but they looked like youuuuuu." The malped's eyes were glowing as it stared at Stella. His body was a gray color that picked up the cold dampness that enveloped them.

"What did you say?" Stella demanded.

"I know the pathhhhhh…"

"No! Who looked like us? What happened here?" Stella yelled.

"How do you know the path, but don't know what happened in this place?" Ebert added.

The malped circled slowly around Stella and Ebert and sat. The tapping of its feet stopped abruptly.

"We have seen ones like you before. But they are gone nowwwwww," the malped replied.

"Other Trebors lived here? Ebert asked.

"I only know they looked like youuuu," the malped looked more closely at Stella as it spoke.

"The tales were true? Other Trebors?" Ebert's voice quivered.

"That must mean the stories of evil are true then," Stella whispered.

"No evillllll...hisss..."

"Please malped, tell us what you know," Stella begged.

"Lightening...a storm....no more fields of treeeeees. Only half the tree left to die...ones like you are gonnnnnnne."

Stella's mind raced as she tried to understand what the malped said. Ebert's nose twitched; fear reflected in his eyes.

"I only know stories toooo...hisssss.....I found this as you seeeee it," the malped retorted.

"We are saffffffe....Pullll that," the malped continued.

Stella followed his line of sight. She noticed a latch on a board on the platform floor. She knelt down and carefully pulled the latch. She heard a click. "Pulllllll..." the malped hissed. Stella yanked and a hatch door opened. She peered inside.

"Ha! It's a slide. Ebert, look, it's an enormous slide."

Ebert moved to his sister's side and looked down the hatch. He took a step forward, but Stella grabbed his arm and pulled him back.

"Wait. Hold on," she said. She turned to the malped. "Where does this lead?"

"The path startsssssss herreeeeeeee…"

"The path goes under the mountain?"

"Yes… underrrrr… hissssss"

Stella glanced at Ebert for his okay, and he slowly nodded yes. She smiled at him and relief swept through her that she didn't have to make the decision alone. She now knew Ebert had more to offer than she had realized before.

"How about if I go first? You give me a minute head start and then follow?"

"Right," he replied.

Stella sat and swung her feet over the opening. She gave herself a shove. Woossshhhhhh! The slide was steeper than she expected, and she caught speed quickly. Her back pressed hard against the slide by the force of her speed. Her hair flew wildly behind her and her breath caught in her throat. Red lights streaked past her face like bolts of lightning. Ebert's laughing and screaming caught in the air above her and mingled with a high screeching sound that made her eardrums thump. Then the steep pitch of the slide slowly eased, and Stella's body relaxed as she came to a stop. Her feet dropped off the end of the slide and she jumped up. In front of her, the malped stood silent and still.

"How did you…?" she began, but Ebert leapt off the end of the slide and jumped in front of her.

"That was incredible!" he squealed.

Stella nodded and looked back at the malped. It cocked its head at her and then turned. Stella shivered and shook off her question.

"Thisssss way…" the malped hissed.

"This way to the path or the way you think Snu might have gone?" Stella asked.

"Bothhhhhh… I think bothhhhhh…" it replied.

They were at the bottom of the trunk now, deep inside its vast, hollow shape. The inside wall of the trunk had two large openings that cast sharp shadows onto the ground in front of them. They were wide and tall with arches on top that looked like they were dug out of the gray granite that covered Mt. Bor. A freezing rush of air blew from the arched holes, and the cold mixed with a bitter stench that gathered all around them. Dark tunnels stretched behind the huge openings away from the core of the trunk they now stood in. Stella strained to see what was ahead in the tunnels, but she could see nothing. Ebert pulled on the hem of her shirt and whispered, "Snu's stone is red."

Stella had never seen the stone turn red before. She grabbed it from Ebert to take a closer look. Red.

"What does red mean?" Ebert asked.

"I don't know. I've never seen it turn red before, and I've never heard Yapa or any of the other elders talk about guiding stones turning red."

"Red is blood," Ebert blurted out. "Blood is bad. This isn't good, Stel."

"Stop it! Stop," Stella urged. As thoughts raced through her head on what the red guiding stone could mean, she felt a wet trickle run down her leg. She looked down to see that the wound on her knee had reopened. A small line of bright, red blood ran down her shin. She shivered and pulled her pack from her shoulders. She yanked out a canteen of water and poured it over her knee. Red water slowly streamed down her leg and into the dirt. The malped leapt away from the stream. Her stomach lurched as she closed the canteen and heaved the pack on her back. A deep ache spread under her ribs. Ebert stared at the ground at her feet but did not comment on the dark crimson ring of mud.

"Come on," Stella muttered and kicked the muddy ring with her foot, smudging away the stain.

"Red, Stel, red. And the stories of their being other Trebors were true. How do we know the malped is right? What about the darkness and evil?" Ebert asked.

"It's too late now, we have no choice to go forward and hope that part is not true," Stella replied.

They forced themselves to walk through the opening and into the tunnel. Within a few feet, complete darkness surrounded them, feeling like a curtain had been pulled behind them, sealing off all light. She put on her headlamp, which sent a bright stream of light into the long dark space. She searched for the source of the terribly potent smell, a stench like something was burning, but she could not see a fire or hear the crackle of flames. Ebert lifted the front of his shirt to his face and buried his nose deep into it, holding it there while they walked.

"How do we know Snu picked this tunnel and not the other?" he asked from behind his shirt.

"We don't. We hope," Stella replied. She felt unsure of herself; her chest tightened and the gnawing in her stomach intensified.

They walked in a gloomy silence, the cold and darkness stealing their words from them. Underfoot, the soft dirt shifted to hard rocks that jutted up from the ground, forcing Stella and Ebert to keep their heads lowered so they wouldn't trip and fall. Icicles clung to the stony cover above them and spider webs clumped in corners, tangled and untouched. Every few minutes the pitter patter of the malped's feet would echo louder. Sometimes the sound seemed to be joined by others, but only two red eyes glowed in front of them, urging them forward. Eventually they came to a wall, and Stella threw up her arms. "A dead end! You led us to a wall, malped!" she bellowed.

"No… hisssssss… small…" it replied.

Ebert squatted down and brushed his hands across the stony wall, while Stella shone her light for him. He felt the crevices of the rocks in front of him until his hand slid off into a small opening. Stella leaned forward and stuck her head into the opening; her headlamp illuminated a small space that led on through the tunnel. The malped's tail brushed lightly against Stella's fur as it quickly maneuvered through the hole. Once on the other side, all Stella could see again was its red eyes. She and Ebert looked at each other, and Ebert shrugged his shoulders and dropped to his knees. He bowed his head into the hole, dropped to his stomach and began sliding along the earth. Stella watched as his feet slowly pulled away. Then she heard him yell, "It's wide open on this side. It looks like rocks just fell into the tunnel causing this block."

"Okay," Stella said. "I'm coming."

Stella removed her pack and shoved it through the hole. Ebert grabbed the other end and pulled it to him. When she swung her hair behind her, something tugged her head back sharply. Stella reached back and found her hair tangled with a mess of spider webs. She ran her claws along the webs, but they were sticky and latched onto her fur. She yanked harder but her hand also stuck in the almost invisible strings. She huffed and turned her head to see if she could untangle herself more carefully. The mess that bound her hair and hand together did not seem too strong. She extended her claws to slowly untangle herself.

"What's taking you so long?" Ebert called.

"I got stuck in a web… I'll be right there," Stella said. She pulled harder on the tiny threads. The fur on her other hand got snagged in the mess and she pulled harder, feeling angry and frustrated. Something soft landed on her head right above her headlamp. With her hands and hair stuck above her all she could do was move her eyes to see what it was.

Spider!

Stella screamed and yanked as hard as she could. Instead of freeing herself, her hands became more entrenched. The black spider lifted a hairy, spindly leg and set it on her nose. Another leg reached over and landed on her cheek. Then another on her other cheek. One by one, the pointed legs ambled over her face until the soft, dark under belly of the spider rested on her nose. A cold thread dropped on her skin. The spider scuttled along Stella's cheek, dragging the thread with it.

Ebert slid back through the hole. When he saw Stella, now encased in thread, his mouth dropped open. The spider lifted Stella from the ground by a tiny, smooth string. Stella's feet grazed the rocks underneath as her body lifted up.

"Shine your lamp towards the spider," Ebert yelled.

Stella did, and Ebert glimpsed the shimmery web. He jumped up and caught the web in his hand and then pulled it to free his sister. But his hand didn't come off; it stuck. Ebert hung by his hand. His stomach smashed into Stella's headlamp, and the space around them went dark. They struggled together to free themselves, but the creepy legs of the spider continued to make circles around them, wrapping them within its silk until soon they were cocooned together in a shimmery white wrap. Then the spider climbed away, leaving them swinging in the dark.

Ebert began to shake violently and laugh hysterically. His head stuck out of the cocoon, while Stella was trapped inside, still pressed against her brother's body.

"Can't find you Yapa, can't find you Snu," Ebert cackled in a sing-song voice. He was losing it. "We're stuck in a spider web!" Stella ignored her brother's insane babble as she tried to struggle free. She couldn't even get her claws to retract in or out. Ebert stopped laughing.

"What? What do you see?" Stella asked.

"Malped!" Ebert exclaimed. "Do something!"

The malped's feet pitter-pattered from Stella's feet then all along the length of her body. It climbed up her slowly.

"Teeeeeeth," Stella heard the malped say.

The cocoon began to shake. Ebert spit. It shook again then stopped.

"What's happening?" Stella yelled.

"It's working," Ebert said.

"What? What are you doing?" Stella felt frantic.

"I'm using my teeth," Ebert mumbled. "To free us."

The pattern started again. Shaking. Stop. Spitting.

"My arms are free," Ebert yelled.

Stella's heart beat more quickly, and she tried to move her arms again.

"Stop, Stel. It makes it harder for me."

Stella waited, still and silent until the sound of Ebert's heavy breathing reached the top of her head. Air. Light popped back into the dark cavern from the now freed headlamp. Immediately, Stella joined Ebert and started to gnaw at the threads that held them. The red eyes of the malped jumped from above her and loomed just below their feet. Stella and Ebert worked quickly. Stella looked up and realized that the black body of the spider had awakened, and it was moving towards them.

"Faster!" she yelled.

They ripped and yanked at the edge of the thread with their teeth. The spider crawled closer. They worked as fast as possible, until Ebert dropped from the web, hitting the ground with a thud. He stood and started to gnaw at the threads on Stella's feet. The spider drew closer. Just as the spider released a new web of silk, Stella and Ebert's work met in the middle and Stella fell free. Immediately, the malped glided through the hole. Ebert followed and Stella dropped to her stomach and inched through as quickly as she could. On the other side, they worked together to push a rock over the opening and stopped the spider. They stepped backwards, away from the hole. Ebert tripped as his foot hit something and he careened over backwards. Stella reached her hand out to help her brother up. She saw a faint glow below his feet. She pulled Ebert to sit up then knelt down by his feet. Her heart skipped a beat.

"Snu's lamp, his lamp! He must have come this way!" she exclaimed. She picked up the lamp for Ebert to see. He didn't look. Ebert was pointing away from them, towards the tunnel's wall.

"Look…" Ebert's voice cracked. Stella tilted her head to see what Ebert was looking at, and then she saw it, too. A foot… still as stone.

Ebert began to shake. Stella dropped to her knees and crawled towards the foot. The floor of the cavern was dark and cold; when Stella reached the foot, she was too scared to touch it. "What if it was Snu's…?" she thought. She held her breath to listen for breathing nearby. She heard no noise. The foot did not move. She crawled closer.

Snu.

CHAPTER 10

Stella found Snu tucked inside a cave within the wall of the tunnel. His body lay on its side on the cold, damp floor. As she moved closer, Snu moved, rocking back and forth slowly and muttering something she couldn't understand. Her heart drummed fast in her chest and a lump formed in her throat. He was alive!

"Snu, I'm here. It's me—Stel," she whispered.

Snu opened his eyes. He swatted at the space between them. A loud, guttural noise came from him, like an animal moaning.

Stella grabbed his hands. "It's me, Snu. It's me," she said again. His hands and arms went slack and his body slumped. Stella rubbed his hands with hers and drew her nose close to his.

"What happened to you?" she asked cautiously, tilting her head further towards him. She searched his huddled shape, trying to see how hurt he was, tentatively leaning closer to him as she looked.

"Red, red… they are coming," Snu murmured.

Stella sat Snu up. "Snu, I'm here. What hurts? What happened?"

"Am I alive?"

"Oh, Snu. You are alive! You are alive," Stella wailed.

"Did you see them?" Snu's voice turned gravelly and he shivered.

"See who?"

"Eyes. *Red* eyes. They see everything!" Snu whimpered. Stella felt a panic rise inside her as well. She grabbed his hands and he recoiled. His hands were so cold, and they felt hard, even his fur was rough and stiff. Stella pulled them closer to her face. In the light of the headlamp she saw they were gray. His claws were dull black, not their usual brown and they looked like stone. She leaned in closer and saw that his eyes were glossy and distant. He didn't blink. Stella waved her hand in front of his eyes. Snu did not respond.

"Snu, can you see me?" Stella tried to ask calmly, but panic crept up her chest and restricted her throat.

"I only see blackness," he replied, as he rocked back and forth. "Except the eyes… I can feel them on me. Those eyes are going to kill me," Snu yelled, rocking harder and faster.

"What hurts Snu? Tell me," Stella tried.

As Stella studied Snu, the pain under her ribs grew more intense. She grabbed her stomach and peered around her for her pack. Something was really wrong with Snu. It wasn't just his eyes that scared Stella, but something inside him was turning dark, too.

"Ebert," she yelled, "I've got Snu. He's okay but needs help. Push my pack to me."

Stella heard Ebert moan as he slid the pack through the space towards Stella. She yanked it onto her lap and reached inside. She grabbed a handful of leaves. Her fingers tingled. Ebert began to sing quietly, and the notes squeezed their way into the air surrounding Stella.

"Close your eyes," she instructed. Snu closed his eyes. Stella slowly rubbed a leaf on each eyelid. At first, Snu flinched and tried to pull away, but soon he stopped resisting and sat still. Stella then placed a leaf in the palm of each of Snu's hands. She told him to close his hands around them and squeeze. She moved to his feet and rubbed the leaves slowly on his frozen skin.

"What are you putting on me? It feels so good," Snu murmured. "I can move my hands again. What is it?"

"Leaves… from our tree…"

Snu furrowed his brow but did not say anything. He took the leaves from his hands and rubbed them on his eyes again. When he stopped, he blinked a few times and now his green eyes danced. "I can see you!" he whispered.

Stella threw her arms around Snu and pulled him close. He lifted his arms and wrapped them about Stella, hugging her tightly back.

"It worked!" Stella whispered in Snu's ear as they hugged. "The leaves are healing you!"

Snu squeezed Stella harder before he pulled away. His wide face stretched into a strange expression, and then suddenly he took a leaf and threw it in his mouth. Stella stared as Snu's jaw moved up and down. Little by little, the grayness that had set into his skin pinked; his limp fur became supple, and his nose twitched. The grey patch around his eye returned to its vibrant color. Stella took Snu's hands in hers again, and they were no longer frozen. They were warm and soft. She waved her hands in front of Snu's face and he laughed. She laughed too; he was going to be okay. Still her stomach seized with a pain as she laughed, and she grabbed her side to stop it. Snu furrowed his brow again. Then he ripped another leaf in half and handed it to her. Stella put it in her mouth and grinned at Snu as she chewed. The leaf tasted sweet. Her mouth tingled. When she swallowed, a cool sensation slid down her throat and into her stomach. It was as if tiny butterflies flew in her stomach. Stella giggled, the noise of her laugh echoing around them.

"Why are you laughing? Is Snu okay? I'm scared out here, Stella, and I can't see the malped anymore!" Ebert whispered into the cave.

Suddenly aware of Ebert, Snu quickly crawled from his hiding place towards Ebert's voice. "It's okay, Ebert. I'm okay. I'm coming," he said.

As Stella watched Snu, relief swept over her. The pain in her stomach subsided, and she was grateful for its absence. She still couldn't shake the uncertain feeling that lurked under her skin, or the loneliness that burrowed deep down, despite having Snu back with them. She knew why. *Home*, she thought, *the tree*. The leaves had saved Snu and were helping Stella; they were the only thing that gave them the strength they needed. Now more than ever, Stella understood the comfort and safety of the tree, the power it had to protect and strengthen the Trebors. She wanted to be back with the other Trebors, back in the safety of her home, back where she wasn't alone or afraid. A new determination filled her. They had to get back to the tree, only with the strength of the tree at her core and her fellow Trebors with her could she ever be of use in finding Yapa and the others. It wasn't just about her anymore, it was bigger than that, and she exhaled as she let the reality settle in of what they needed to do next.

CHAPTER 11

They sat collapsed against the tunnel wall, Ebert and Stella flanking Snu, with their arms and hands intertwined. The only light came from Stella's headlamp, which flicked every few moments and threw shadows into the cold space. Ebert rubbed the grey streaks in the fur along Snu's arm. He smiled as his long fingers worked up and down, both giving and taking comfort in the action.

"Why were you yelling about the eyes?" Ebert asked quietly.

Snu's body stiffened. Ebert moved his fingers more quickly, but Snu remained rigid.

"Did you see the eyes, Ebert?" Snu asked, his voice harsh and imploring.

Ebert responded quickly, "We saw eyes, too. Lots of eyes. It was scary but then they were good. They helped us escape when we fell through that hole in the trunk. You don't have to be scared of them, Snu."

Stella squeezed Snu's arm as Ebert spoke, trying to reassure him that Ebert's words were true, but Snu pulled his arms away and rubbed the top of his head furiously.

"You don't understand. Either of you. Those eyes were evil, and they are near. I know it. We're still in grave danger."

"Don't say that, Snu," Ebert mumbled. "We are together now. We'll be okay."

As Snu turned to Ebert and then to Stella, he shook his head. Words tumbled from him, "I was panicked when you fell through that hole in the tree trunk. I screamed for you, but I didn't hear anything. All I could see inside was black. I even shone my light into the darkness, but I couldn't see anything either. There didn't seem to be any bottom to the hole. I crawled into it, but as I began to climb down, I was surrounded by winds that felt like a tornado. I could barely hold on. The space around me glowed and pushed me up. I couldn't climb down. I had to go back out of the hole. I was so scared, so worried."

As Snu spoke, his eyes became glossy and he wrung his hands roughly. His breathing became shallow and uneven. Stella wondered if he knew she and Ebert were still there.

"*Stella! Ebert…* stella, ebert, stella ebert… my echo… just an echo… where are they? *Stella! Ebert…* stella, ebert, stella, ebert. The force of the wind is too great. I can't climb anywhere. I can't get to them. *Stella! Ebert…* stella, ebert, stella, ebert. *Answer me! Where are you? Are you okay?* okay… okayyyy. There has to be another way in. Run. Around the trunk, again. Run again, around the trunk. Another hole? Another opening? Nothing!"

Snu's body twitched, his head shook.

"Snu, it's okay. It's over. We are here," Stella said, but Snu seemed lost in his story, trapped in the awful memory.

"I can't give up. There has to be another way. Stop crying, stop screaming, you have to focus. Save them. Wait. What's that? Something is scratched into the bark. A leaf? What happens if I touch it? A door! A door. Maybe this is another way into the trunk—maybe it will lead me to Ebert and Stella. I have to try. There is no wind. I can step in. *Stella*? *Ebert*? I've lost them forever. Pull that latch. A slide. Just go. The board just slammed behind me. So fast. Can't breathe. Must be getting closer to where they fell. I'm coming. I'll find you. I must be getting closer. It's so cold and I can't see anything. *Stella*? *Ebert?* Red dots. Everywhere. Getting closer. On me. Run! *Stella*! *Ebert*!"

Stella crawled in front of Snu and shook him hard. His head shot up and he looked at Stella. Recognition spread across his face.

"You are here with us now, Snu," Stella whispered.

Snu nodded and rocked slowly back and forth. Stella put her arms around him, and they rocked together. Ebert rested his hand on Snu's back.

"I thought I'd lost your forever. I thought you were dead," Snu muttered. "Until I heard your voice in the cave, I didn't even know if I was still alive."

"But you are. We all are. You're here with us, now," Stella repeated.

They rocked together.

"We saw lots of red dots, too. You don't have to be scared: they were eyes, the eyes of malpeds, just like the one guiding us. There are hundreds of them. They took shelter in the trunk from the storm. You can't see their bodies because they camouflage to black and only their eyes show," Stella explained.

Snu stopped rocking. Stella dropped her arms, and Ebert moved in front of Snu to sit facing him.

"They are good," Ebert added.

"They were all around me, all over me. I tried to stop them, to grab one, and when I finally did, its body was scaly, and it hissed. You are saying they were all malpeds? The red dots all belonged to malpeds? If that is true, then the malpeds are evil because what I touched, what my hands grabbed was evil!"

"They are not evil, they helped us Snu," Ebert tried again.

Snu stared at Ebert and raised his eyebrow. "I squeezed it and it exploded in my hands. It exploded into more red dots. They started to get closer and closer together and then all of the dots merged into two red dots. But they weren't dots. They were eyes. They merged into eyes. They stared at me. I was hit on the back and knocked to the ground. Everything went dark… I couldn't see… I could only feel an icy cold breeze all over me. I crawled to get away from it. My toes were freezing, and I was losing feeling in my hands. I kept crawling until I felt an edge. I crawled along the edge until I found the place where you found me. I didn't move until you came."

"That can't be right," Ebert whispered.

CHAPTER 12

"We can't go back the way we came. If we go through that hole, we could end up back in the webs," Stella said. She had managed to calm down Snu and reassure Ebert, and was eager to move.

"You came from that way?" Snu asked and pointed to the rock that blocked the hole Snu and Stella had crawled through.

"We put that rock there to stop the spider. Long story, but I don't think we should go back the way we came. I don't know how we'd get back up the slide either," Stella said. "Ebert, you didn't see which way the malped went?"

"Why won't you listen, Stel. Forget the malped. The malped is bad. It's good it's gone."

"You don't know that the big eyes you saw have anything to do with the malped. He helped us find you," Stella replied.

"I know what I saw. I know how I feel. They have to be connected somehow. Those eyes, they came when I was hiding in the cave. I couldn't see them, but I could feel them. I knew when the eyes were near because my insides felt like they were turning to ice, and pain shot through every inch of my body. We need to move before they come back."

"Okay. Let's move. This way," Stella pointed down the tunnel ahead of them. The light from her lamp made the damp walls glisten.

"That takes us the opposite direction from where we came," Ebert said.

"Yes, but I think we are now under the mountain. Look at the tunnel walls. They are stone, not wood like the trunk walls at the beginning of the tunnel. The path to the other side of the mountain must be under the mountain, that's why the malped was leading us this way. It's our best chance to get out and back to the tree."

"What about Yapa?" Ebert asked.

"After we get out of here, we can climb up the back side of the mountain and hope the others see us on the mountain path and come for us."

"And then they'll send help," Snu said, suddenly understanding Stella's plan. Stella nodded.

Snu clutched his chest suddenly.

"What's wrong?" Stella asked.

"The pain is back. They're near," Snu whispered. The fur on the back of Stella's neck stood up as he spoke. "The pain in my chest… the cold… the terrible cold. The eyes are near. We are in danger. We have to hide." Snu's voice was urgent and his eyes darted from one side of the tunnel to the other. He grabbed Ebert's hand and began walking quickly down the tunnel. Ebert clung tightly to Snu. Stella noticed that with his other hand, Ebert turned the guiding stone over and over again. It was a vivid red. When they stumbled on a rock, Snu dropped Ebert's hand and clutched his chest again. He fell to his knees. Stella ran to Snu's side and pulled him back to his feet. She peered around the tunnel for somewhere to rest and then half-carried Snu to a nearby corner. Snu had a distant look in his eyes. He was breathing heavily.

"We have to get out of here," Stella muttered under her breath. Snu stared into the dark tunnel ahead of them.

"What are you looking at, Snu?" Ebert asked.

"Shhh... don't speak. It's there. It's coming," Snu replied, though barely loud enough for Stella and Ebert to hear.

Ebert's little body began to shake. His eyes grew big and round. She shifted him behind her and opened her pack to pull out some more leaves. Snu grabbed her hand and shook his head.

"They help you," she whispered. "It worked before."

"No. Save them. Until we get out of here this is going to keep happening and we don't want to use them all up. What if you or Ebert need them?" As Snu leaned over to pull the zip closes, he froze. The malped was sitting on the pack, its body still, and its little feet pulsated.

"Helloooooo Snuuuuuuuu... so happy you are okayyyy... hissss..."

"Malped! Where did you come from—where were you?" Stella roared.

"I wentttttt for my friendssssss." The malped replied. "They have come to help you..."

Stella noticed that red eyes covered the tunnel walls. At the edges of the beam from her headlamp she could vaguely see the outline of their bodies, but their skin matched the walls, so their eyes once again looked like flying dots. Her heart skipped a beat. She was breathing heavily. Snu finished zipping the pack and stood with great effort. He glared at the malped and shook his fist.

"Was it your friends here that tormented me? I've seen these eyes. They haunted me! How can you tell me you are here to help!" Snu spit the words out.

"We are good. We will guide you. You have nothing to fearrrrrr…" the malped replied calmly, but his voice sounded deeper and more urgent.

"We don't have time for this, Snu. If something bad really is here, we need to get out. Malped, is this the path under the mountain? Will this get us to the other side of the mountain?" Stella said.

"Yesss…." the malped hissed.

"We will follow you out. Show us," Stella said.

"*Nooooooo!*" a voice boomed.

Ebert screamed and wrapped his arms around his head. Snu grabbed his chest and lunged forward.

Stella realized that the other malpeds had disappeared. The voice seemed to come from the hole behind them. "You said this path was easy, malped. Take us through it and out to the other side of the mountain. Malped. Malped?"

The malped was nowhere to be seen. He had vanished along with the rest of the malpeds. Stella grabbed Ebert's hand and began to run. Snu stumbled behind them, grabbing at his chest. Ebert tripped as Stella pulled him and she found she was dragging him, tugging at his thin hands. His claws dug into her hands, but she kept running faster and faster.

"*Stop!*" It was the voice again.

"Run! Faster! Hurry," Stella yelled. She couldn't see more than a few feet ahead. She hoped the tunnel would end soon. Her heart raced. Her breath was short and shallow. She plunged forward through the tunnel, willing herself forward.

"Stop, Stella! Stop," Ebert yelled. "Snu…" Stella stopped and glanced over her shoulder. Snu lay on the ground.

"What happened?" she asked as she squatted next to him.

"My feet. They are frozen. I can't move them. Go! Get out of here," Snu demanded.

"We are not leaving you," Stella cried.

"*No, you are not leaving!*" the booming voice was drawing closer.

"It's the eyes, or whatever it is. It's close and it's coming. Run!" Snu yelled.

The space around them turned icy cold. Stella snatched a handful of leaves from her bag and shoved them at Snu. "We are not running without you. What good will the leaves be if we aren't even around to use them?"

Snu didn't blink as he stared into Stella's eyes. He nodded once. He placed the leaves in his mouth and began to chew furiously, shoving his other hand in his pocket. Within a few seconds, his color was normal again, and he was on his feet. Stella and Snu each grabbed one of Ebert's hands and began to run towards what looked like an opening at the end of the tunnel.

Then they saw the glow in front of them. The red eyes loomed just beyond the tunnel's arch. A freezing gust of wind blew into the them, knocking them off their feet. They scrambled backwards on the ground, their feet slipping beneath them as they tried to gain traction and stand up again. When Stella got to her feet, she yanked Ebert up by his armpits. Snu leapt to his feet and they turned to run in the opposite direction. As they ran, cold bit at Stella's back and clutched at her heart. As she sprinted through the tunnel, she could sense the red eyes behind her, closing the gap with every step. Ebert's feet gave way again and Snu grabbed the little Trebor and heaved him onto his back. Ebert shrieked as they ran, his face buried in Snu's back.

Ahead Stella saw the rock that covered the hole to the other side of the tunnel. She pushed herself to run even faster, envisioning herself pushing the rock aside and squeezing through the passage before the eyes caught them. As they reached the rock, Ebert screeched with panic. Stella swung around to see Ebert being pulled from Snu's back. Ebert's arms were wrapped so tightly around Snu's neck that the blood was draining from Snu's face. Ebert's legs were stretched behind him as if they were floating. Clamped around Ebert's feet were shadowy fingers. The fingers grasped tightly to Ebert, the glare of the headlamp revealing scaly skin. Behind the hideous hands, red eyes hovered.

"Let him go!" Stella yelled, and ran towards the eyes.

"*No!*" The voice boomed.

A blast of glacial air blew Stella backwards. Her body hit a tunnel wall. The stone around her crumbled. Another gust blew into her, propelling her through the crumbling wall and into a vast open space. She flew through the air until she smashed against another wall. The space was enormous and bright. The walls were rough granite that climbed thousands of feet high to form a tall peak.

Snu hit the wall next to her and slid to the ground. They both jumped to their feet and ran back towards the tunnel. Before they could reach it, Ebert appeared, his tiny body engulfed in the grasp of a giant, scaly hand. The hand changed from black to the gray of granite as it moved into the light of the space. An immense arm followed, also shifting in color as it entered inch-by-inch.

"Help!" Ebert screamed.

The '*hisssssss*' that came from the tunnel behind him drowned out his screams. Stella and Snu picked up rocks. They threw them at the arm, screaming and yelling for it to let Ebert go. Another arm reached through the hole, its hand ending in three, long, scaly fingers with huge circles of loose skin hanging from the tips. The hand swatted away the rocks, which ricocheted back at Snu and Stella. They ducked to keep from being hit.

Red eyes. Stella saw them. Two enormous, bulging eyes that blazed red as fire. Around the eyes, an immense round head slowly formed. The skin, the same granite color as the arm, was covered in scales. The scales glistened as the enormous creature cocked its head. Its voice boomed, "*Stop!*"

Snu and Stella stopped throwing rocks; their arms fell limp by their sides. They stood in awe as the rest of the creature's enormous body crept from the tunnel and materialized in front of them. Stella gasped when she saw its body; her chest tightened, and her stomach lurched. The creature looked just like the malped, but enormous and frightening. Everything about it was the same as the malped she had come to know, except it was huge and hideous. The creature wore a spiked crown, the only thing that remained black. Its huge body circled around them, its giant tail dragging behind, its hundreds of feet thundering as it formed a ring around where Stella and Snu stood. The creature held Ebert in its hand high above them. A cloud of cold air settled in the space. Stella, Snu, and the giant malped stood perfectly still. Ebert's cries pierced the air as he struggled, dangling hundreds of feet above them.

The giant malped cocked his head and looked at them, its stare was hard and fierce. Snu slowly moved closer to Stella and took her hand. He squeezed it hard. Stella realized she hadn't been breathing and as she let out a long exhale, her breath sent a misty, white cloud streaming into the cold space that enveloped her.

"Let him go," she yelled. The giant malped cocked its head in the other direction in response.

"Do you understand me? Let him go!" she shouted. Ebert's feet swung wildly in the air above her. He groaned.

The giant malped pulled its long tail and feet in closer, tightening the circle that surrounded Stella and Snu. The feet began to drum in a rhythm around them. The sound was not a pitter patter, but the sound of thunder ringing around them. Stella and Snu covered their ears to muffle the noise. The giant malped stretched its head down towards them, halting a few inches from their faces. The thundering stopped. Its nostrils flared and it exhaled a gentle but freezing gust of air into their faces. Stella reflexively pulled her hands from her ears and wrapped them around her chest and arms. Her bones rattled and her teeth chattered. Light reflected in a blinding glare off the black crown atop the giant malped's head. Stella's head began to throb. Snu moaned beside her.

"You want him?" The immense malped's whisper was a deep, scratchy singsong.

Stella nodded.

The giant malped pulled its face away and lowered Ebert until he was in front of them, hovering a few feet from the ground. Ebert's body was gray and limp, and his eyes drooped shut as his head lolled to the side.

"*Ebert*!" Stella screamed and lunged towards him. The giant malped swatted her hard, sending her to the ground. Snu leaned down to her, slipping his arm under her back to sit her up.

"What do you want with us?" Snu asked.

"Finally, you ask the right question," the malped replied. It dropped Ebert from its grasp. Ebert fell to the ground in a heap and made no noise. The giant malped backed away and sat still. Its eyes bulged. Its scaly skin glistened as it sat and stared at them.

Snu leaped towards Ebert as Stella scrambled to her feet and followed. They rolled Ebert onto his back, but his eyes stayed shut.

"The leaves. We need the leaves," Stella screamed hysterically. "But I've lost my pack." She felt Ebert's face, which was ice cold. She began to rub his arms and body quickly. Snu lifted Ebert's head.

"What are you doing?" Stella cried. "You need to warm him. It's the only way We've got to get the cold out of him."

Snu reached into his pocket and pulled out two leaves. He placed the leaves in Ebert's mouth and began to move his jaw back and forth, and up and down. Stella sat back on her heels and watched. Ebert's nose twitched; his eyes opened, and he blinked at her. Snu sat Ebert up and the gray color slid from Ebert's face.

Ebert managed to mumble, "Thank you." Stella smiled and Snu squeezed his shoulder.

"YESSSSS…*That is what I want*," the giant malped's voice echoed next to them. "Those leaves are what I want."

Snu turned to the giant malped. "That was the last of them. We have no more."

"You will get them for me. You will get me *more*."

"Snu, where did you get those from? Do you have more in your pocket?" Stella asked as quietly as she could.

"I only ate one when you gave them to me before. I saved these, just in case," Snu replied.

"So you have no more? Even if we find my pack, the ones I gave you were the last I had." Stella said.

"*You will get more!*" The malped's voice was loud now. Its feet began pounding again.

"From where? We have no more!" Stella demanded.

The pounding feet stopped, and the giant malped rushed its face within a few inches of Stella again. "You will go back to the tree, you will gather leaves, you will get sprouts, you will take the new growth, and you will bring it to meeeee." The feet thundered up and down another time. "I will show you the way out. You will go home, and you will bring me back what I have demanded. I will find you if you do not—you and your loved ones will die if you do not do as I ask."

"I…." Stella's voice broke as she spoke.

"*That is not all!*" the malped bellowed.

"OKAY," Snu yelled. "We will get you the leaves! What else could there be?"

"After you have gotten that, *I want the tree dead!*"

Stella dropped her head. Ebert slid his hand into Stella's. "We can't kill the tree. It's our home," he whispered.

"I know," Stella replied and looked back to the giant malped.

"We can't do that. We can get you what you need, but that is our home. We can't kill it."

"*Can't* or *won't?*" the giant malped roared.

"Both!" Snu yelled.

"*You will do it!* You will put poison on the tree's roots, and it will die slowly. The Trebors will have time to move. You will move here. You saw the old homes. Why do you worry? You already left the tree—you turned your back on it to come here alone. Now I'm just telling you to finish what *you* started," it said.

"Why? Why do you want us to do this?" Snu asked.

"Because I am the king. *I am the king!*" The malped's voice grew louder with each word, and its feet began to thunder again. Its whole body moved now, circling around and around. Stella and Snu tried to speak but their words were lost in the noise that took over the great space. Stella put her hands to her ears.

"I want that power for myself. I shall rule!" The malped lifted its great tail and swung it, pinning them to the ground and holding them there. The tail coiled around them tightly; Stella felt like she was being squeezed like a snake's prey. They could not move. They gasped for air. The giant malped leaned in and blasted them with cold as it hissed, "*Do it, or perish!*"

Stella tried to free herself, she tried to reach for Ebert, but every part of her body was paralyzed by the outrageous tail. Her breath became more labored and her eyes could not focus. Her head felt light and darkness gathered at the edges of her eyes.

"Okay," she managed to squeak out before darkness took over.

CHAPTER 13

Muffled sounds came to Stella as she lay in darkness. As if underwater, the sounds floated above her, garbled and faint. The darkness felt comforting. The voices were a lulling invitation to sleep. Soon the voices grew louder and clearer. Snu. Ebert... calling her. Urging her to leave the muted darkness. *Open your eyes Stella.* Stella slowly opened her eyes. Snu's face was concerned; Ebert's was covered in tears. Both noses twitched furiously.

"Stel, Stel! Can you hear me?" Snu asked.

Stella nodded and propped herself up on her elbows. She looked around for the giant malped, but it was no longer near them. She scanned the space until her eyes settled on the tunnel entrance. There she saw red eyes and shivered. She scrambled to her feet.

"What happened?" she asked.

"You said, okay!" Ebert whimpered.

"Okay?" Stella furrowed her brow and looked at Snu.

"You said okay to that monster's demand. You said okay, and it released us and moved away back to the tunnel." Snu tilted his head towards the eyes in the tunnel.

"I thought we were dying. I didn't know what else to do," Stella explained.

"It was the right thing. It was the only way out. Doesn't mean we have to follow through," Snu whispered.

Stella turned to Ebert. She brushed the tears from his cheeks and gave him a weak smile. His nose twitched.

"I wish we never left our tree," he said.

"Me, too," Stella replied.

"But what about Yapa? If we leave, we can't help him," Ebert said.

Stella felt her chest clench. "We have to get home, Ebert. Yapa will be okay. I was wrong to think we could do this alone. We need the others to be able to help Yapa."

"But he could still be in trouble... and..."

"*Brave* Ebert. Trust us. This is the right thing to do. We all have to be brave together," Stella interrupted.

"What is that?" Stella noticed a small vial of black liquid on the ground in front of her.

"That giant monster dropped it there when it released us. It must be the poison," Snu said.

Stella picked up the poison and put it in her pocket. She walked towards the tunnel where the red eyes lurked, her heart thumping hard in her chest. She could hear Ebert's heavy breathing and Snu's deliberate steps behind her. The eyes disappeared suddenly, and she stood still.

"Stella... hissss..."

Standing alone in front of an entrance to another tunnel was the tiny malped, his small feet moving quickly, pitter patter, pitter patter. A shiver crept up Stella's spine.

"Commme... this wayyyyyy... I will show you the way out," the malped said.

Ebert ran towards the malped, "Why did you leave us? There is a giant creature and we were in trouble. But you..." He stopped in the middle of his sentence and stared at the malped. His hands trembled. "You... you are just like it but small." Ebert slowly walked backwards away from the malped.

The malped jumped towards Ebert and landed on his arm. It turned the color of Ebert's fur as it climbed to his shoulder. Stella ran to Ebert.

"I look like the giant creature... but I am not it... don't be scaaarrrred..." the malped hissed into Ebert's ear. Ebert looked at Stella and she managed to force a smile to calm him.

"You are evil, malped," Stella spat. "You left us. You knew that giant monster was coming. You are just like it. I don't know how, but you are connected to it somehow."

"Nooooo... hisss... I look like it... but not the same... hisss... I hid because I was so afraid."

"Malped, leave us. Go! We don't trust you anymore!" Snu hollered.

The malped leapt from Ebert's shoulder and glided back to the tunnel entrance.

"We're not coming, malped. How could we trust you?" Stella said.

"Nooooooo... I only want to help... I am not the same... do not go towards that tunnel... do not go towards the eyes... let me helllllp..."

Stella grabbed Snu's arm and pulled him close enough that she could whisper in his ear, "It was the malped that saved Ebert and me in the trunk, when you were hunting for us. Maybe it's telling us the truth?"

"No," Snu hissed.

"It's again our only option, to follow it into the tunnel," Stella said. She did not wait for an answer. She walked towards the malped.

"There is always another choice," Snu muttered. It was too late, though; Stella was determined to escape.

Inside the tunnel, the red eyes of the other malpeds hovered along the walls: eerie, red lights speckling the dark space. The darkness was filled with the pulsing sound of the pitter patter of their feet moving rhythmically against the hard surface. Cold clung to the walls and the space was lit only by the glow of the malpeds' eyes. Stella placed each step in the tunnel with care as boulders littered the floor. Stella, Snu, and Ebert made their way slowly, ducking under rocky overhangs and squeezing through tight crevices. The path inclined at times so sharply that they had to climb, using their claws to steady their progress. As they walked, they breathed hard. As the path wound up and around, each turn revealed more darkness. Stella's legs burned. She huffed through her mouth as she tried to keep up with the malped. Then, through a pin-sized hole, a single string of light fell onto the ground in front of them.

Snu touched the back of Stella's arm and whispered in her ear, "We have been walking up for some time now. I think that faint glow of sunlight comes from the field—it must be our way out."

The eyes of the malpeds were clustered around them more tightly than before. Stella asked quietly, "Do you think if we make a run for it we can get out before that creature returns?"

Snu shifted his weight and looked around nervously. The red eyes hovered so closely that the sound of their feet made Stella's ears thump. The malped had stopped and was standing in the path in front of them; its legs were not moving. It stood still, its head cocked to one side, and its eyes were a fiery red than before. Stella's breathing quickened as she walked on without speaking. The malped turned slowly and again took its place in front of them in the tunnel.

"The guiding stone is hot," Ebert whispered.

Snu took the stone from Ebert and closed his hand around it. He looked at Stella, "It's red and it's hot. I've never known a guiding stone to turn red."

Stella kept walking. The red eyes swarmed close to her in tight bunches.

"It has been red since we came into the trunk, but never hot before," she replied without turning.

"We have to run. We have to get out. The guiding stone is trying to warn us of great danger," Snu said again under his breath. He grabbed his chest.

As Snu spoke, the space around them turned suddenly colder and a rush of wind blew past them. They froze. The malped climbed along the side of the tunnel wall to join the other malpeds, its body quickly taking on the black color of the walls. It was impossible to distinguish it from the other red eyes that hovered around them. The wind picked up intensity and began to swirl, blowing around and around them, getting fiercer with each circle. Stella grabbed Ebert and pulled him to her. Snu stepped in closer to them and looked around frantically.

As the wind rushed around them, it sucked a malped from the wall and its red eyes became part of the spinning. Then another was pulled from the wall, and another. Soon all Stella could see was red whirling around her. Spinning quicker and quicker.

"Hissssssssssss…" the space that surrounded them said as it grew louder… "*hisssss*." Faster, faster, louder, louder, red swirls, piercing hissing. Stella's hair lashed her eyes. She felt sick and dizzy. Red flashes. Wind. *Hisssssssss*.

BOOM!

Around them, the body of the giant malped began to form out of the whirling, swirling red. Enormous red eyes. A scaly face. A black crown. Then the long body and feet, so many feet. The giant malped hurtled around at the pace of the wind. A tornado of scales and red, a tail whipping through the air. Stella screamed and clutched Ebert closer. Snu threw his body on the other side of Ebert, both smothering him between them.

"*You lied*," the malped's voice caught in the wind around them, echoing back in circles. "You lied, you lied, you lied… hissss…"

"I said okay! I have the poison. We're just heading to the tree like you asked. We didn't lie," Stella yelled.

"*I heard you. You cannot outrun me. Now you will perish like the others.*"

The wind circled closer. The giant malped's body moved with it. It pulled Stella, Snu, and Ebert together with its enormous tail and ran down the tunnel, dragging them behind it. Its huge suction cup feet held them so tightly they couldn't move. Everything around them blurred with the speed of the giant creature. The thunder of its feet made it impossible to hear each other's screams. They were back in the cavern again; they had left the tunnel and any glimmer of the light they had tried to reach. The giant malped climbed the steep walls. It rose higher and higher as the trio dangled from its tail, swinging violently back and forth. When it stopped, the scaly tail coiled through the air to hold them up to its face.

"*Perish.*" The giant malped screamed. Its cold breath stung their faces.

It threw Stella, Snu, and Ebert into a hole in the granite wall. They flew through the air flailing, arms and legs everywhere. Stella felt like her chest might explode. She slammed into Ebert and then Snu. They landed heavily. The ground was hard and cold. They were trapped.

CHAPTER 14

"Stella! Ebert!"

"Snu!"

Darkness filled the space around them. But the voices that had come from the dark were bright and clear. Stella's eyes adjusted. Arms were around her; big, strong arms. Hands rubbed her back and pulled her closer. Air returned to her lungs, and she gasped.

"Yapa. Yapa!" Ebert shrieked.

"Yapa?" *Could it be?* Stella snapped her head back and peered into the darkness. "*Yapa*!" She threw her arms around her father. Ebert pushed his head between them. "Yapa," Stella said again, and her voice quivered as she spoke. "How can this be? Where are we?" Stella's head was fuzzy, and tears sprang to her eyes. She gazed at Yapa again, willing herself to believe he was real.

Yapa laughed at her disbelief and the white fur around his eyes fanned into the creases of his smile. He pulled Ebert and Stella closer to him. His eyes also glistened as he held his children tightly.

"My children," he said over and over.

The reality of being with Yapa and safe in his arms was almost more than Stella could bear. Sobs rippled through her body, releasing the stress and loneliness that had invaded her every muscle.

"Shhh… it's okay," Yapa whispered. "We are all together."

Stella sobbed harder. Ebert squeezed his body closer as he silently cried into Yapa's furry white chest.

"How are you here?" Stella finally managed to ask. She sat up to look at her father; Ebert loosened his grip.

"I was going to ask you the same," Yapa replied, humor in his voice.

Chuckles came from the edges of the dark cave. Stella realized it was the others, the elders who had travelled with her father. Snu's father was there. A few feet from where Stella, Ebert and Yapa sat, Snu and his father embraced.

"We came for you," Stella whispered.

"For me?"

"Yes, I thought we could help you, help all of you," Stella said, sweeping her hands through the air. "We were worried you'd been harmed in the storm and we came to hunt for you, to help."

"By yourselves?" Yapa asked.

Snu tried to take some blame. "The tribe was focused on rebuilding, and we didn't want to wait."

"No, it was me. It was my idea, my fault we ended up here," Stella interrupted. "I thought I could do it alone, and these two tagged along. I was so wrong Yapa, so, so wrong." Stella fought to suppress her sobs.

Yapa pulled her back to him to stop her crying; the elders muttered in the darkness.

Stella took a deep breath. "The farther we got away from the tree, the worse things became. Loneliness, doubt and fear took over. Watching Ebert and Snu suffer—well, it's been awful. It's all my fault."

"Oh Stella, I wish you would have stayed at home, with the tree, where you are safe and loved," Yapa said.

"Me, too," Stella wailed.

"My dear Stella, it's my fault you're here. I should have told you the truth before the elders and I left. Perhaps then you would not have come to find us, you would have trusted the tribe and the safety of our tree."

"I don't understand," Stella said.

"We didn't leave the tree, all of you, for supplies. We left to warn any survivors of a colony of Trebors that separated from us years ago. We didn't want them to suffer in the storm. We hoped to bring them home." Yapa said.

"The malped was telling the truth," Ebert whispered.

"I can see now that we have been wrong to keep this truth from you all," Yapa continued. "We thought we were protecting you all from the darkness by keeping the troubles of years past, away from you."

"Then you knew about the giant malped too, Yapa?" Stella asked.

"We have known of the giant malped for many, many harvests past. We have been battling this danger for years. It wants to control the tree. It wants the power for itself. Many times before, Trebors have been tempted to help."

"It tried to force us to kill the tree," Ebert wailed.

"As it did us," Yapa replied. "But when we refused it brought us to this cave and we've been here since."

"But how did it capture you? If you knew there was such great danger, why would you enter the trunk?" Stella asked.

"We did not know if there were Trebors still trying to live in the trunk. Long ago the giant malped persuaded them to steal from our tree. He told them that life would be richer if they controlled the growth, if they each had their own tree to sustain them, instead of sharing one together. But lightning struck down the trees that they tried to grow. They had a whole field of them, tiny trees growing for the individual use of each Trebor. They lived in the big tree at the edge of a field and acted as farmers for their selfish crop. That is, until the day of the lightning storm. The storm destroyed the field, and nothing ever grew there again. It also tore the tree in half, leaving the torn trunk. Their homes were charred and unlivable. Many of them realized how lost they were, how wrong they had been. They came home. We forgave them and welcomed them back, but most of them lived the rest of their lives in the darkness of the dead trunk." Yapa explained.

"And you thought some might still be alive?" Snu asked.

"We did. We entered the trunk to check for them, but before we had a chance to search, the giant malped descended on us and, well, as you can see, we were unable to stop his fury."

"We trusted the small malped; he was our guide," Ebert said.

"I was so wrong to follow it, but it seemed so harmless," Stella added.

"Did the malped lead you to the trunk and into the darkness of the mountain tunnels?" Snu's father asked.

"It told us is was an easier path to the other side of Mt. Bor. I am so sorry, so sorry," Stella repeated.

"I know you are, Stella. It was a grave mistake to leave the tree, but I should have been truthful with you. We are both to blame. You see, without the strength we gather from the tree we are all too weak to resist the temptations and evil that draw us to this dark place. Even we were not prepared enough to travel so far away." Yapa said.

"It's a shock to me that you even made it this far," Snu's father interjected. As he spoke, he leaned in closer to Stella and his gray fur shimmered as he gazed at her.

"It was the leaves," Ebert responded quickly.

"What?" Yapa asked, startled by Ebert's interruption.

"You have leaves?" one of the elders called from the darkness.

"A bird brought them to Stella!" Ebert said.

"You saw the bird?" Yapa asked earnestly.

Stella's cheeks burned. "Yes, but the others didn't. It brought me leaves from home. The leaves saved us."

Yapa clapped his hands together and laughed. He grabbed Stella and pulled her close to him again. Her face smooched against his shoulder, and she felt his shoulders bounce up and down as he laughed.

"You were chosen, my love. You were given a great gift," he said. "No wonder you were able to make it this far."

"The leaves were a gift to all of us. I was dying and they saved me," Snu added.

"It's more than that," Yapa said. "She was able to see what most can't. She saw the flight of the bird."

"But Snu and Ebert didn't see it. Why, Yapa?" Stella asked.

"I've always wondered myself. It seems only when you are truly open can you see it. I saw it first when I was a young Trebor. I was desperate, tired of looking different with this white chest and feeling alone. I called for help, pleaded not to be alone, and it appeared to me. I was young and only told the elders. Until now, no other Trebor has seen its flight." Yapa put both hands on Stella's checks, "You are special my child," he said.

"Indeed," Snu's father added. "But we need to focus on what's at hand now. Where are the leaves?"

Stella dropped her gaze and shook her head no. "We have no more," she said. Yapa's hands fell to his lap. He closed his eyes and groaned, deflated.

"It is okay child. We were just hopeful," Yapa said.

"We used ours, too. We were just hoping that you had more. We used our last today. It is also how we've survived," Snu's father added.

Stella felt the pit in her stomach widen. She fought the urge to cry again. She could not speak and was wrecked that she had nothing to give. She had run out of anything she had to offer.

Snu finished the story that Stella had no strength left to tell. "The giant malped wants them. The leaves," he said. "It wants the sprouts of the tree, and then it wants the tree poisoned. It brought us here when it learned we would not do its bidding."

In unison, the elders murmured their assurances that they had made the right decision to deny helping the evil, giant malped. Without speaking further, Yapa pulled Stella and then Ebert to their feet. He guided them to the back of the cave and pulled a lamp from a pack, which he used to examine Stella, Ebert, and Snu. He looked into their eyes and felt their pulses, then he turned them around, checking each of them carefully, scanning for any marks or injuries. Yapa paused at Stella's knee and placed his hand over the long gash that marked her skin. As he gazed at her, he inhaled and exhaled slowly. Stella could see his eyes were watery. Next, he pulled out a small canteen of water and gave it to her.

"It is our last. Drink slowly," Yapa instructed.

The water was so cool as it slipped down Stella's throat. The liquid eased the burning that had settled deep inside her. Stella shut her eyes.

After Snu and Ebert had all had some water, and Yapa seemed satisfied with his inspection, he spoke again.

"How are the others? Your mother?"

"The tree kept us safe. When we left, it was healing itself before our eyes," Ebert answered. Yapa smiled at Ebert and patted his back.

"What is our plan, Yapa? How will we get out and home to our tree?" Ebert now asked hopefully. Yapa and the elders turned silent. To Stella, it felt as though all of the air had been sucked out of the cave. Yapa sighed again.

"The giant malped is very powerful. When we tried to escape, it got hold of us and threw us back into the cave. We don't have the tools here to defeat it," Yapa replied.

As he spoke, Yapa continued to pat and rub Ebert's back. It seemed to be the only comfort he could give while he shared the dire news. Then his hand stopped; and his head snapped up. Yapa leaned toward Ebert. He pulled at something around Ebert's neck. From under Ebert's shirt came a long, leather lanyard. At the end hung a pouch. Yapa held the pouch in his hand. Ebert dropped his head.

Yapa's voice was very even. "Ebert, how did you get this?" he asked. He pulled at the drawstrings that cinched the top of the pouch shut.

"I'm sorry. I just thought... you left it. I thought it was important because Stella tried to save in the storm. So I brought it with me. I'm sorry, Yapa. I'm sorry..." Ebert blubbered.

"Sorry! Sorry!" Yapa laughed. "This is wonderful!"

As Ebert looked at his father, his nose twitched. Stella snuck in closer to see the pouch. The others did the same. Yapa slipped the lanyard from around Ebert's neck and poured the contents of the pouch into his hand. Tiny, brown seeds fell into the palm of his hand. Yapa held the lamp to them. He extended his hand for everyone to see.

"These are the answer," he exclaimed.

Stella looked at Snu and he widened his eyes; his forehead wrinkled. Stella gave a slight shake of her head and turned back to look at the seeds. It was such a small handful, insignificant. They were round and smooth. She did not understand why they mattered.

"These seeds are poison to the malped, even to the giant malped. They are very small, but very potent. Even the smallest handful can destroy the creature," Yapa said.

Snu's father took a few of the seeds into his hands and rubbed them between his fingers. He smiled and showed them to Snu before he handed them back to Yapa. Yapa poured them all back into the pouch and pulled the strings to seal them safely inside.

"Does the malped need to ingest the seeds for the poison to take effect or can they just make contact with his skin?" Snu's father asked.

"Only its skin," Yapa replied.

Stella's heart raced with joy as she smiled at her father. For the first time since she had started on this journey, she had hope.

CHAPTER 15

Stella was surprised the wild beating of her heart didn't echo off the cave walls, alerting the nearby giant malped. Instead, the space around her was so quiet it made her ears ring. She swallowed several times to keep her fluttering heart from disrupting her thoughts and from halting her courage. Stella and the others had to work together now if they wanted to defeat the giant malped, if they ever wanted to return home. Yapa had run through the plan with everyone, over and over. It would work, he had said, it had to. But Stella's fear and uncertainty grappled against her father's assurances. She stood at the cave's edge wondering if the tiny bit of faith she had would be enough for what she had to do next.

"Is everyone ready?" Yapa whispered from the darkness behind her. She knew Ebert was next to Yapa but she couldn't see either of them. Yet, though she couldn't see her brother, she knew he was as scared as her, as she could feel his shaking in her own bones. Snu lurked on the other side of the cave's opening. He peered into the cavernous space. Granite towered miles above them and climbed for miles below. The chill in the air pricked Stella's nose and spread frost across her fur. She opened her hands. She rolled the seeds around in her hand three times and then squeezed her fist shut again. She took a step towards the cave's edge and glanced towards

Snu. He nodded. Stella swallowed again and stepped away from the wall. She now stood in the middle of the opening where there was nothing but cold, harsh granite and a punishing fall in front of her.

"Now, Stella," Yapa whispered.

Stella froze.

"Stella," Yapa said again, more urgently.

Stella jolted and stood more upright. It was time.

"Malped," she yelled. *Malped, malped, malped....* Her voice echoed. "We have found fellow Trebors in this cave," *Cave, cave, cave...*

"But they're not well," she continued. "They need help. I will do everything you have asked so that I can get them help. Please." *Please, please, please...*

Stella waited. She watched the abyss beneath her, expecting to see the giant malped climbing up towards her.

"Malped! I will do it! I will get the leaves, and I will poison the tree. Just let me help these Trebors." *Trebors, trebors, trebors...*

Thundering, pounding—the giant malped was coming. Cold gusts rushed through the cave opening. Stella stood still and tall. The monster's thundering steps made the granite rumble, and huge boulders spilled from the peaks. Everything shook. Stella bent her knees to keep from falling into the pit in front of her.

"*Hissssss...*"

The sky rained debris as the walls shook.

"Stay the course," Stella heard Yapa yell through the thundering.

From the corner of her eye, Stella saw Snu grab his chest and lean forward. Fear seized her. The giant malped was near. Her knees buckled, but she shifted quickly to catch herself and focus ahead.

Within moments, Stella stood face-to-face with the scaly, dark monster. It blew curly, cold blasts of air into her face. Her eyelashes froze instantly as the giant malped leaned closer to her, inches from her face. Her breath caught in her throat as the cold took over her lungs.

Black sludge dripped from the malped's garish crown, and its red eyes bulged so far from its head they seemed to float above its skin. The skin was the color of the granite; and the rocks that fell around it were lost in the camouflage as they bounced off its immense body. Spikes encircling the malped's face were tinged with red at the points. The spikes glowed like embers before Stella's face. The giant malped's long body and tail hung into the abyss below them while it rested its scaly arms at the cave's opening. Stella's hands convulsed and she couldn't stop herself shaking.

"*Yesssss…* hisssss… you will followwwww meeee… hissssss," the giant malped bellowed.

"Now," Yapa yelled.

Stella narrowed her eyes.

"*Never!*" she screamed.

She raised her hand above her head. She reached back and threw the seeds at the malped's face with all of her might. They scattered, spinning through the air as they flew towards the giant malped. One struck the its face and melted into its skin. A white film spread across the evil malped's gray face. The other seeds missed their mark, but the single seed was all that was needed. The giant malped screeched and jerked back, pulling away from Stella, moaning and screaming. Snu wound up from the side and threw another seed. It struck just above the great beast's eyes, spreading another white rash.

The others rushed up beside Stella and Snu to throw more seeds. One by one, the seeds spread white through the malped's skin. The giant malped roared and moaned. Soon most of its body was covered in a sickly, white crust. Another screech ripped through the air. The giant malped lost its grip on the granite wall. The floor beneath the Trebors rumbled and shook as the enormous malped pulled off fists full of granite as it struggled to catch a hold. Suddenly it was tumbling head over heels into the hollow space. Its deafening roar made the granite walls crumble as it plummeted to the ground. With a thud, the malped landed. The impact ricocheted throughout the space, sending debris everywhere.

"Let's go! Now. This is our chance," Yapa yelled.

Yapa threw Ebert on his back and began climbing down from the cave. Stella, Snu, and the others followed. They scrambled quickly, scraping their claws into the granite walls as they climbed. Stella stayed close to Yapa and Ebert. Snu climbed steadily with his father. The other elders silently descended behind them. Eventually, their feet touched ground, and Stella pointed to the tunnel entrance where they had seen the pinpoint of sunlight. Snu ran towards it as the other Trebors followed.

As they reached the archway, the giant malped stirred. It raised its great body from the ground and screeched. The sound made the inside of Stella's ears burn. Yapa pushed her into the tunnel and swung Ebert from his back, propelling him towards Stella. Snu's father grabbed Ebert's hand. He nodded to Snu to do the same, and they pulled Ebert hard yelling, "Run, run children."

The Trebors sprinted through the tunnel. Stella's legs burned as she struggled to keep up with the group in front of her. She stumbled, reached out her hand to break her fall, then quickly pushed herself back to her feet. The giant malped's scream tore through the air again. Cold air snatched at their backs.

Yapa yelled into her ear as they ran, "Keep running, don't stop! Keep running no matter what."

Stella's heart raced. Her steps faltered, but she kept moving. Up they ran, up, closer to freedom, closer, up. Finally, she saw the light, the tiny stream of hope. *Faster, run,* she thought. Yapa panted next to her. Ahead, Snu and his father dragged Ebert. In front of them, the elders pushed boulders away from the hole. Rock by rock they forced an opening. Then Stella saw the field. Bright sunlight. Ebert and Snu burst into the field. Stella's stride quickened, but a sharp chill froze the back of her neck. Her fur stood on end all along her arms.

"*Run!*" Yapa yelled, his voice strained. Stella turned to her father as she ran.

"*No!*" she screamed.

Yapa's face was contorted. His eyes wide. A white, stony hand encased his body.

"*Run!*" he yelled again. Red eyes loomed in the tunnel behind. Stella lurched out of the tunnel entrance. The bright light startled her, and she covered her eyes quickly. She raced towards the middle of the field where she could see Ebert, Snu, and the others.

"It got Yapa," she yelled.

The giant stood in the field. Its body was now completely white, except for its red eyes and black crown. It clutched Yapa in its stony hand.

"Use the final seed, now," Yapa pleaded.

Stella's hand fumbled in her pocket. She pulled out the final seed, the one they had decided to hold back in case they needed it. She held their last hope in her hand.

"Now Stella, now," Yapa yelled again.

Stella threw the seed at the giant malped. As if in slow motion, it travelled through the air, all hope pinned on its flight. It struck the malped between the eyes. It screeched and dropped Yapa. Yapa's body rolled under its feet. The giant malped lifted its stony arms into the air and all at once its legs crashed to the ground. The ground shuddered. The malped's shoulder tilted and began to crumble. White boulders dropped from its body as it fell towards the ground. An avalanche of malped hit the earth with such power that smoke rose from its form. Fire leapt from the pile of rubble. Heat billowed out from the giant malped with a force that sent Stella back to the ground.

"Yapa!" she screamed.

The Trebors ran towards the fire and the remains of the monstrous malped. Yapa was trapped underneath. They began yanking at the stony rocks, burning their hands as they pulled at stones that had formed the giant malped. Flames blazed hotter and higher, singing Stella's fur. Ebert screamed, and Snu's father pulled him from the fire's edge. Snu grabbed Stella by her shoulders and heaved her away from the rocks.

"It's no use. You'll burn," he yelled.

"No! Yapa..." Stella wailed. She twisted away from Snu and lunged towards the rubble, but the fire was too hot; she could not get close enough to pull at the rocks. Snu and his father dragged her from the fire.

"No. We can't give up," Stella spat. She ran around the field, frantically searching for something that could help them.

"Stop, you have to stop," Ebert pleaded.

"It's not too late. If we work together, we can save him!"

"Child, your father knew the sacrifice he was making when he told you to use our last seed. He knew that it was the only way to save us all," Snu's father said.

"The power of the tree, it can do anything. It saved us from the storm. It could save Yapa," Stella yelled.

"We have nothing left of the tree with us. We have run out of options," Snu said.

"Together, if we believe together in the power of the tree and each other I know it can save Yapa!"

Snu hung his head and Ebert whimpered next to Stella, taking her hand in his. Stella realized she was crying.

"Please," she pleaded. "Believe me. If we ask for help and trust it to come, it will."

Stella peered into the sky. It was so blue and clear with no evidence of the carnage that surrounded them, or of the pain that seared Stella's heart. She knew there was more they could do. Deep in her soul she knew if they believed together, they could save Yapa. She closed her eyes and thought of the tree, remembering the strength it showed in the storm and the graceful way it healed itself. She thought of the tiny Trebor who sang so boldly during the storm, and the memory made her feel warm. Her heart fluttered. And so, she sang.

She filled the air with her uneven tune and ragged words; she let her heart sing. A gentle breeze blew across her singed fur and she sang louder, stronger. Ebert squeezed her hand and sang, too. Next

Snu joined. Stella opened her eyes. A stronger wind blew past them, and the burning fire crackled as the wind swept over its flames. Snu's father joined the song and soon the other elders lifted their voices in a chorus to the sky. Stella's pulse quickened. It was coming! There, in the sky, it was coming. She dropped Ebert's hand and pointed in the distance. She sang louder. The wind picked up around them and blew towards the fire. The fire blazed higher, fighting the torrent of wind. In the sky above, the current carried a swooping, circling, red and yellow bird. Every Trebor saw it and sang at the top of their lungs. They waited and watched as the majestic bird approached, its mighty wingspan blasting the air with an even greater rush of wind. The wind was so great that it whooshed over the fire and blew it out.

As the fire smoldered, the bird swept gracefully over the stony form of the giant malped. It dropped leaves from the tree over the pile of rubble while it glided. Then the bird landed on the rubble. Soot rose from the stones and into its wings. The bird shook the filth from its feathers and bowed its head towards the stones. A green current swept from its beak and across the giant malped, cooling the stones. Stella raced towards the bird. She reached out her hand to touch the stony malped. It was cool. The bird shoved a huge piece of the stony malped from the pile and it rolled off the mountain of rubble and into the field.

"Together, together we can free him," Stella yelled.

The Trebors joined Stella and, stone by stone, they pulled away the tomb that encased Yapa. They worked in silence, afraid of what they would find, though stronger than they had ever been before. They worked together to move the mountain that buried Yapa. After pulling an enormous, white boulder from the pile, they saw an opening. The stones gave way to reveal a cave within the mountain of debris. Stella pushed her hand into the hole to see how deep it was.

Fingers greeted her; a hand slid into hers.

"*Yapa*!" she screamed. "He's alive!"

The Trebors furiously pushed aside the remaining stones. Yapa lay in the middle, unscathed. He reached out his arms and the elders pulled him from the hole. Stella threw her arms around her father and Ebert jumped on top of them. Snu and his father wrapped their arms around the small group and one by one the other elders did the same. They hugged, laughing and crying.

The bird stood above the Trebors, still and calm as they embraced. The shimmer of its feathers stood in stark contrast to the barren form of the giant malped. It sang a single note. Stella rose to her feet and raised her arms up towards the bird. It lowered its head, resting its beak on the ground in front of her, its blue eyes sparkling. Stella caressed the crest of feathers on the bird's head. The bird remained very still. She pressed her face against the bird's feathers. They were warm and soft. As she ran her fingers through them, a spray of colors shimmered, a bright and cheerful rainbow of feathers.

"Thank you," she said.

"Do you think it can carry us home?" Ebert whispered.

Stella gazed directly into the bird's clear, vibrant eyes. She knew the answer was yes. She walked back to the bird's neck and carefully reached up to grab hold of the crest of feathers and pulled herself up, swinging her legs over its back. Ebert and Snu ran to the side, and Snu boosted Ebert up while Stella pulled him onto the bird. Yapa, Snu's father, and the others hurried over to climb aboard the bird. Then the bird lifted its head, turning it from one side to the other. A gentle wind caught the feathers around its face. Stella leaned forward and grabbed hold.

The bird unfolded its great wings and flattened its back as its head tilted forward. Lifting its wings, the bird shot up into the air. Wind rushed over Stella. Her heart leaped in her chest. It pushed higher with its wings and then held them outward where they caught the breeze, easing them into the current, drifting upward. Ebert's face glowed and he grinned as they flew. Snu's lips were tight but the sides of his mouth turned up. Yapa cried with joy.

Below, the shape of the giant malped grew smaller and smaller, its massive form seeming insignificant from the bird's back. They circled in the sky above the field a few times before the bird lifted its wings and throttled downward, away from the field, away from the giant malped and the darkness of the mountain.

"We are going home," Ebert yelled into Stella's ear. "Home!"

CHAPTER 16

Ahead the tree reached like a beacon into the sky, strong and beautiful, bathed in green. In the days that had passed the tree had completely healed itself. Where branches had been torn, there was now new growth. Where leaves had been ripped away, there were now bold streaks of green. Even miles away from the tree, Stella could see its branches reaching high, the green of its leaves up and down its huge trunk. As the Trebors on the bird flew closer, the fullness of tree took Stella's breath away. She smiled as they glided through the sky. Below, the forest still lay barren, but a circle of green on the forest floor radiated out from the tree. From the sky the green seemed to creep along the ground from the roots of the tree, like ripples from a pebble thrown into a pool of water. The yellow of the evershi flower rode the ripple of green, dotting its hue with its bright, shy petals.

The bird flew higher as they got closer to the tree, soaring above its tallest branches. Circling in the sky above, the bird rode the currents of wind. The tiny shapes of Trebors surrounded the tree below, and many of the Trebors began to climb. Up along the tree's trunk, along its branches, Trebors climbed; their faces coming into focus the higher they scaled.

"They see us!" Snu exclaimed.

Ebert waved with one hand while his other grasped feathers. He laughed as he waved. The Trebors below waved back. As the bird circled closer, the sound of their cheers rose into the air. The bird swooped down and flew around the tree, and then did it again, around and around it went. Cheers greeted them. The happy faces of friends and family whirled past as everyone yelled and waved furiously. The Trebors on the ground below began to separate, creating an open space on the green forest floor. The bird hovered in the space above the opening, its wings rippling in the breeze. Its clawed feet hung below them as it descended into the opening, pulling in its wings, propelling its head up. Stella held on tightly with one arm over Ebert as they landed. Whoops and hollers filled the air. Trebors crowded the bird, each reaching out to touch its feathers, laughter taking over. It seemed that everyone raised their hands to them. Stella carefully slid Ebert to the crowd. He travelled from her hands to the hands of the other Trebors, laughing and smiling.

Snu turned to Stella, "You next," he said. Stella laughed and leaned into the hands stretched out to her, letting her body slide from the back of the bird. Her feet touched the ground and she was instantly surrounded. Snu and the others were nearby being smothered by the welcome of the Trebors. Beside her, her mother knelt on the ground, her arms engulfing Ebert. She reached to Stella and pulled her towards them. Stella collapsed into her mother's arms and Yapa threw himself into their embrace.

"I love you. I love you," Stella's mother muttered over and over again.

"Oh, Yama," Stella cried, "I'm sorry, I'm sorry I left..."

"It's okay my child. You are home. That's all that matters," she whispered.

Stella's body sagged. She felt suddenly exhausted, as if all the energy had drained from her body. She was home. She lifted her eyes to look at the crowd around her. Each face reflected back acceptance and love.

The bird raised its wings and then took to the sky. It circled over their heads as its song filled the air. Stella, Ebert, Yama, and Yapa clung to each other, their tears flowing. A small voice joined the song of the bird. The sound was quiet, sweet, and flawless. Soon a chorus surrounded them. The voices of the Trebors filled Stella's ears, she felt a flutter in her heart and a small smile pulled at the corner of her mouth. She sat back from her family and lifted up her face. Yama and Yapa began to sing with the others, their voices full of joy and hope. Stella could only mouth the words. She was overcome with emotion. She closed her eyes and thought of her journey. She thought of the storm, the giant malped and her loneliness, and then she thought of the bird, the tree and her home. She felt peace and she felt loved. She opened her eyes and found that the song was now coming from her, too.

CHAPTER 17

Stella woke before her family and quietly made her way out of the tree. The morning light bounced from the green that spiraled its way from the tree, casting a glow against Stella's skin. Stella still couldn't believe all that the Trebors had done to rebuild while they were gone; or the healing that the tree had done. She saw with fresh eyes the power that flowed from the tree and how it had saved and sustained all that lived in it. She couldn't wait for everyone to wake up so she could now join in on the singing and dancing. She could now be part of the work to recover what had been lost in the storm. She never wanted to miss out on the time together again. Letting the gentle breeze of the morning sweep through her fur she looked to the tree.

"Stella, what are you doing?" Ebert's voice made Stella jump. "I woke up and you weren't there. You aren't leaving again are you?"

Ebert stood in the shadow of the tree's great entry. Behind him Snu leaned out into the morning light.

"Snu?" Stella asked.

"Ebert saw you were gone and came for me," Snu replied. "Don't do it Stella, why would you leave?"

Stella threw back her head and let out a happy laugh. She skipped forward and pulled Ebert and Snu to her.

"I'm not leaving," she spoke quietly to them. "I'll never leave the tree again, or try and do it all alone. You, the tree, and all the Trebors, are my family, my home, I belong here and never want to leave."

Ebert exhaled and picked up his head to look at Stella. She ruffled his fur and he giggled.

"You are different Stel," Snu said.

Stella grabbed Snu's hands and squeezed them tightly. She looked into his eyes and then let her gaze drift.

"I was so wrong," she said.

Snu dropped her hands and picked up her chin so their eyes met again.

"In the end, you were the one who saw we could only survive together, you were the one that called for the power of the tree. You saved us because you didn't try to do it alone. Stel, do you see that?"

Stella sniffled as she tried to hold back her tears. The three once again embraced. They were so close Stella could hear Ebert's heart beating. Slowly, they unraveled, and she smiled at them, overwhelmed with love.

"So, what are you doing then?" Ebert asked.

"I was going to look for the bird," Stella replied. "I wondered if it would ever come back."

As she spoke, a gust of wind blew through the clearing. Leaves from the forest floor swept into the air, forming a small whirl of green. They watched as the green spiraled into the sky. And there above them, they saw the vibrant colors of the bird. It circled overhead and its song drifted down to them.

"It's back," Ebert whispered.

"Yes," Stella replied. "Yes, I see it now, I understand it now, it was always here, with us at the tree, it's just now we have eyes to take notice of it."

The bird rested its body on the top branches of the tree and settled its head to rest. It looked so peaceful as if it had been there all along. Stella, Ebert and Snu watched it for a moment more and then linked arms and together walked back into the tree.

SNEAK PEAK OF TREBOR TALES, BOOK 2

PROLOGUE

Dusk clung to the sky as darkness pulled at the corners of the horizon. The air was still, thick and smelled rancid. The white form of the stony giant lay in the field and the dark of the night that settled into the sky shrouded its body. The shape of the giant had crumbled into a pile of stone that now only held the smallest echo of the terror it had once caused. Coldness seeped into the field, engulfing the space with its bite.

Then, it appeared.

Tiny, slithering, silent.

Another joined it, oozing from the form of the dead giant.

They moved quickly, low to the ground, smooth and deliberate. From every hole, crack, and opening more appeared. Like water pushing its way out from an underground rapid, they sprang and flowed out of the dead giant. But they did not take the form of water, they did not reflect the sparkle of the moon as it rose in the sky, they were not fluid. They were dark and they skittered around, escaping from the hidden places that hung under the dead form of the giant.

Thousands of tiny, dark creatures flowed into the field, their presence consuming the space. A low hiss caught in the wind. The sound carried across the field mingling with the smell of death that seemed to run alongside it. They began to move, scrambling on top of each other, climbing, slithering, running. They moved across the opening, gaining speed as they scurried towards the dead tree trunk that stood at the corner of the field. They took over the trunk, climbing up its side, racing around it, again and again. Then, just as the sound of the hissing and the smell of rot became too much to bear, they slowly disappeared. One by one, they stole into the trunk, their shadows escaping into the hollowness of it. The field was silent once more. The dead giant in its pile of rubble now looked cold and lonely again, still and forgotten. Until suddenly its white surface reflected a red glare, bouncing color from its stony skin.

From the trunk, shooting from its top, a red mist sprung into the air. It hung in the sky over the field; the colored haze lifting to the sky. Fog rolled into the space and the red glow hung on it, seeping into the dusky air, taking over the field and everything in it.

And that was how it stayed for a long time…red, rancid, and silent.

Made in the USA
Middletown, DE
05 June 2020